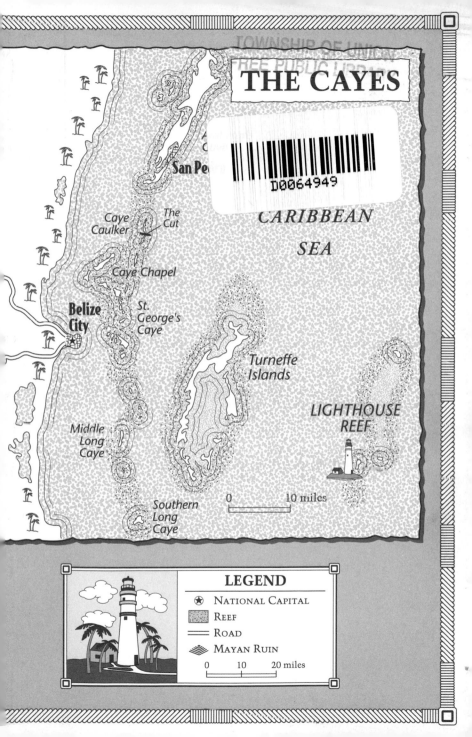

THE CAYES

San Pe...

CARIBBEAN

SEA

Caye Caulker

The Cut

Caye Chapel

Belize City

St. George's Caye

Turneffe Islands

LIGHTHOUSE REEF

Middle Long Caye

Southern Long Caye

0   10 miles

LEGEND

★ NATIONAL CAPITAL

▦ REEF

═ ROAD

≋ MAYAN RUIN

0   10   20 miles

DANGER ON
LIGHTHOUSE
REEF

PASSPORT
NO. 4
MYSTERIES

DANGER ON
LIGHTHOUSE
REEF

P. J. STRAY

Silver Burdett Press
Parsippany, New Jersey

Published by Silver Burdett Press
A Division of Simon & Schuster
299 Jefferson Road
Parsippany, NJ 07054

Designed by Leslie Bauman Design

Library of Congress Cataloging-in-Publication Data
Stray, P.J.
Danger on Lighthouse Reef/by P.J. Stray
p.cm.–(Passport mystery:#4)
Summary: When teenage twins Maddie and Mike visit their
engineer father in Belize during spring break for his wedding,
they become entangled in the mysterious sickening of the sea
animals around the reef at Caulker Caye.
[1. Belize–Fiction. 2. Twins–Fiction. 3. Remarriage–Fiction.
4. Manatees–Fiction. 5. Mystery and detective stories.]
I. Title. II. Series: Passport mysteries: no. 4.
PZ7.S9136Dan   1997   96-48171   [Fic]–dc 21 CIP   AC

Printed in the United States of America
(LSB) ISBN 0-382-39774-6   10 9 8 7 6 5 4 3 2 1
(PBK) ISBN 0-382-39775-4   10 9 8 7 6 5 4 3 2 1

$10.00

JM
STR
C.1

10 - 98

CHAPTER
1

"It's a big mystery," Mike and Maddie's father, Steve Richards, declared, running his hand through his short brown hair. "The animals on the reef are acting very strange. We haven't got a clue about what's going on." He sounded frustrated.

The taxi they sat in was hot and stuffy as they waited for traffic to move. Maddie wiped her face with the white lace handkerchief her mother had given her before the plane took off and looked over at her twin brother, Mike. He responded with his "gotcha" look and leaned toward his father who was sitting in the front seat next to the driver.

"Dad," Mike asked, "why aren't we moving?"

Her father turned around and smiled. "This is a traffic jam, Belize-style. Twice a day Swing Bridge, the big bridge up ahead, is opened to let boats and ships move up and down Haulover Creek. It usually takes only a few minutes. Otherwise things move along pretty well. Once we're out on the ocean you'll feel cooler. I promise."

"I'm glad we found you at the airport, Dad," Maddie said. "We were getting a little nervous."

Their father smiled at her. "I'm glad you found me, too."

When Mike and Maddie had landed at Goldsen International Airport outside of Belize City, their father was nowhere to be seen. It was the first time that the twins had flown alone, and it was such a long distance. The crew of the airplane had been very nice, but Maddie had worried about going to a whole new country—not to mention having to meet their Dad's fiancée. Their parents had separated three years ago, mostly because Dad's job took him away from home so much. Now he was working in Central America, doing something with coral reefs. Their mother was a lawyer for a big firm and her work kept her in the city.

Outside the taxi, jeeps and trucks, along with a large crowd of people on foot, waited patiently for the bridge to close. In spite of the heat, people seemed to be enjoying themselves. Music blared, with different tunes mingling and drowning out each other. People smiled at one another and gathered in groups to talk and laugh. The cabdriver waved occasionally to a passerby.

Most of the brightly colored buildings along the road were only two stories high—three at the most—and their shiny tin roofs gleamed in the sun. Many of the buildings were covered by vines with huge golden flowers shaped like trumpets or by bright red or purple flowers that drooped over their porches and open balconies. Palm trees towered overhead, swaying gently in the afternoon sunlight.

"On that side of the Creek," their father said, pointing across the river, "is the shopping area. This side has the hotels and some of the nicer houses."

Mike looked at an old wooden building sitting next to the road. "How come there aren't any tall buildings, Dad?"

"There are a few, but people have to be careful of hurricanes down here. Tall buildings can be pretty dangerous."

"We get a big blow about every thirty years or so," the cabdriver added. "One in 1931 and another in 1961 did serious damage. Looks like we're just 'bout due for another."

"Is that true, Dad?" Maddie asked anxiously. "Could we get caught in a hurricane?"

"No, Maddie," her father replied. "Hurricanes

don't come in any pattern. Besides, it's the wrong time of the year. That's why I wanted you to come down for spring break. April is one of the nicest months to visit here."

"Spring break *and* the wedding," Maddie thought, but she kept it to herself.

Mike was still peering at the buildings along the road. "Those walls look pretty thin," he commented. "How do they stay warm in winter?"

Maddie made a face at him. "Duh! There is no winter down here," she said. "We're in the tropics."

"You want an umbrella?" a man asked, sticking his head though the open cab window next to Maddie. He had dark black skin and a friendly smile, but she shied back in surprise at the way his head had just popped into the taxi window.

"You want an umbrella?" the man asked again. "Soon it's goin' to rain." He was grinning broadly. "Look at those clouds!" The clouds were piled up offshore over the Caribbean, white and fluffy at the top, but dark and ominous at the bottom.

"No, thanks," their father responded, showing him the umbrella he had with him in the front seat. "We're okay."

The man smiled again and pulled back. He had umbrellas of all kinds lined up along one arm, hanging by their curved handles. He reached into a back pocket with his free hand. "Maybe you need some fine postcards," he said, pulling out a small stack of cards and handing them toward Maddie.

"Go on now, Rafe." the cabdriver said. "These aren't tourists here."

The man in the street peered at Maddie and Mike's father. "Yeah, Mon," he said finally. "I know this man. You're the engineer that's been working out on Caye Caulker." He pronounced it "Key Corker."

Mr. Richards smiled. "I'm the one," he replied.

"They say you're goin' to give us a lot of jobs," the man continued.

"I'm trying."

"But bad things are happenin' out there. People say the fish are actin' crazy, swimmin' in circles. What you think about that?"

"Rafe," the cabdriver said before Mr. Richards could answer, "go on now. Don't be bothering the engineer."

Rafe smiled and bowed slightly, "Proud to meet you, Mr. Engineer. Maybe you can figure out that problem and give me a job some day. Just remember Rafe's a hard worker." Then he moved back along the line of cars, trying to sell his umbrellas.

The cabdriver looked at Maddie and Mike's father. "People talkin' about you, sayin' you're buildin' oil wells out there. Maybe that's what's makin' the fish crazy."

Mr. Richards shook his head. "No. The team I'm on is trying to develop a system to make drinking water out of seawater. Nothing we're doing should bother the fish."

"Water?"

"An endless supply of drinking water could make all the islands in the Caribbean livable," Mr. Richards replied. "We're trying to use the coral to filter the water over the reefs."

"Dad's an oceanographic engineer," Maddie chimed in. She always smiled when she thought of that word—oceanographic. It sounded pretty exotic and exciting.

The cabdriver brushed his arm across his brow. "But coral is just some kind of rock."

"Not really," Mr. Richards responded. "Coral is a living colony of millions of animals that gradually builds a reef out of the skeletons of earlier generations. Healthy coral catches tiny bits of food out of the passing currents of water." He scratched his head. "That's where the mystery comes in. Your friend Rafe is right. The fish on the reef are acting very strange. We're finding some fish where we've never seen them before and others that should be there have disappeared. And the ones that we do see are acting peculiar, swimming around strangely and acting confused. The biologists on our team just can't figure out what would make them act that way. It started happening only a few weeks ago. Something is affecting the reefs, something mysterious."

The cabdriver turned toward Steve Richards. "Lots of fisherman 'round here are out of work. Folks got to catch fish to eat. If the fish are sick, we'll be sick."

"That's why we've got to solve this mystery," the twins' father replied.

There was a commotion on the road. "It looks like we'll be moving soon," the cabdriver said, peering ahead.

Maddie's father glanced at his watch. "Do you think we'll make the ferry to Caye Caulker?"

"No problem." The cab jolted ahead.

CHAPTER
2

The water was smooth and clear as the small ferry approached the open ocean. The boat bounded over the ocean swells, heading toward some small islands. Mike stood with his legs apart, trying to keep his balance as the boat shifted in the water. "This is awesome!" he said with a smile.

Maddie sat next to her father on a wooden bench at the back of the ferry. A group of men sat further forward, playing cards. One of the men had a radio that was playing loudly. The others shouted to be heard over the music. The noise bothered Maddie, but her father didn't seem to notice. He pointed out some of the sites in Belize City off to their left as they sped past. The sun was low in the sky, giving the buildings an orange and pink color. Many houses were built right on the water and had pretty white fences. Some had docks jutting out with small boats tied beside them.

"Pretty nice, huh?" Maddie's father said over the roar of the boat's engine. She nodded in agreement. The color of the buildings and the trees made the city look like some of the magical places in her books back home. Maddie thought for a moment about her room, her books, and her collections, but she knew it was best to put that right out of her head for now.

Then there were fewer houses, and the coast became a long band of emerald forest, with palm trees and thick brush.

"Doesn't anybody live out here?" Maddie asked.

"Those are mangroves," her father replied. "Most plants can't stand the salt water but mangroves can. They grow right into the sea, and fish use them as a kind of nursery to protect their young. The young fish hide from predators among the roots."

The boat hit a swell and bounced, throwing Mike off balance. He tumbled against the bench, but caught himself. A splash of spray came over the side. The men up front laughed loudly.

"We'll be there in about forty minutes," their father said. "The ferry stops at St. George's Caye before Caulker."

"What does caye mean, Dad?" Maddie asked.

"It means a small island. Farther north we call them keys."

"Like the Florida Keys?" Mike asked, trying to stand straight as the boat lurched again.

"Right," their father replied. "That's how they pronounce the word here, too, even though it's spelled c-a-y-e."

The engine became quieter and the boat slowed, then the engine roared. The boat lurched to a stop as the propeller churned the water behind it, spinning in reverse. Mike reeled backward, then staggered forward, tripped and fell in a heap on the deck. His father stood up to help him. One of the men shouted toward the pilot house and the others laughed.

"I'm okay," Mike said, looking more stunned than hurt. "What happened?"

His father pulled Mike to his feet. "We stopped short for something," he said, but I don't . . ."

"Dad!" Maddie called. "Look there!" She was pointing toward the water in front of the boat. An ominous gray shape appeared just below the surface for a moment, then disappeared beneath the swells.

"It's a shark!" Mike said excitedly. He gripped his throat with both hands. "It's Jaws! Coming to get you, Maddie." He grabbed for her shoulder, but the boat lurched again, making him miss.

"How would you know?" Maddie replied. "You've never even seen a shark."

"I've seen them in movies and at the aquarium. That's definitely a shark. A big one!"

"No, it's not," Maddie retorted. "It hasn't got a fin."

The gray creature surfaced again, slowly rolled over, and disappeared beneath the ocean swell. Maddie was right. The creature didn't have a dorsal fin like a shark.

"It's a whale," Maddie guessed.

"A killer whale," Mike teased.

The gray creature surfaced again, only a few feet from the boat. Its head rose up out of the water and it peered at them with large black eyes.

"It's a manatee," their father said.

The manatee held steady in the water and kept its head and shoulders above the surface. Its face was deeply wrinkled and ancient looking. It had a huge gray muzzle with a downturned mouth and bristly whiskers around it. Its black eyes were shiny and seemed to be staring straight at the twins.

"It looks like the walrus at the zoo," Mike said.

"Except without the tusks," Maddie added. "It's so ugly, it's beautiful."

CHAPTER
3

The twins and their father stood at the side of the ferry looking at the manatee. The men from up front crowded around them.

"This is very strange," the twins' father said. "That manatee shouldn't be out this far. Manatees usually stay close to shore."

The manatee floated upright with its head out of the water, still staring straight at them.

"What's it looking for?" Maddie asked.

"I don't know," her father replied, shaking his head.

"It's looking for dinner," Mike said to Maddie, "and it's staring straight at you."

Maddie cringed for a second, then crossed her blue eyes at her brother. A man in a blue and red striped T-shirt squeezed in beside them to get a better look.

"Cut it out, Mike," his father said. "Manatees are one of the gentlest creatures on earth. They only eat grasses. That's why they never come out this far. There's no food for them this far from shore. It's too deep."

"That's a big one," the man in the blue and red striped T-shirt remarked, "big as a cow."

"He's right actually," Mr. Richards said. "Manatees used to be called sea cows. They can weigh as much as three thousand pounds."

"Feed a family for a week," the man in the blue and red T-shirt said. "Too bad we can't fish for them."

Maddie shuddered.

One of the crew members shouted up to the captain and the boat's engine roared. Then the engine settled down, and the boat moved ahead very slowly. The manatee stayed where it was, bobbing slightly in the ocean swell, gradually turning its head to follow the boat. The group of men went back to playing cards.

"That was good of the captain," the twins father remarked.

"Slowing down?" Mike asked.

"Yes. Manatees are an endangered species. Several are killed by boats each year and many others are cut by propellers. They can't swim fast enough to get out of the way."

Maddie smiled thoughtfully. "They sure have cute faces."

"Cute?" Mike responded. "They're too ugly to be cute."

"It's interesting you would think that, Maddie," her father said. "At one time manatees were thought to be one of the most beautiful creatures in the world. Sailors thought they were mermaids."

"You mean those women with fish tails and long flowing hair?" Mike said in disbelief.

"Yup," his father replied. "Sailors saw manatees from far away, sitting up in the water the way that one is. They thought they were humans swimming. The story probably got better each time it was told, and soon the manatees became beautiful mermaids."

As the boat pulled farther away, the manatee leisurely rolled over and dove beneath the surface of the water. "Look!" Mike shouted. They could see long white scars on the manatee's back.

"That one's been hit by a propeller," a crew member remarked. "It's lucky it didn't get killed."

"Do you think those men would have killed it if they could have?" Maddie asked in a low voice to her father, pointing to the men playing cards.

Her father looked at the men, seeming to notice them for the first time. "They're just out-of-work fishermen, Maddie. They know they're not allowed to kill manatees. They'd go to jail."

As the manatee was left behind, the boat picked up speed. Soon several small islands came into view. "That's Caye Caulker." The twins' father pointed to the island nearest to them. "There's the Turneffe Islands off to the right and Lighthouse Reef farther out. You can snorkel there."

"It doesn't look like anybody lives there," Mike remarked as they approached Caye Caulker.

The shoreline was lined with a thicket of green shrubs reaching out into the water with no sign of buildings or people. "More mangroves," his father replied. "You'll see the town in a minute."

Soon several docks appeared, jutting out from the shore. A variety of boats were tied to them, mostly fishing boats, but also some expensive-looking sailboats and powerful motorboats. Beyond the docks they could see the small town, a collection of houses built on stilts above the sand.

"Cool!" Mike exclaimed. "It looks just like *Gilligan's Island*."

"You've been watching too many old TV shows," Maddie replied, but Mike was right. The town looked like a movie set with sandy streets and brightly painted houses. "Why are the houses on stilts, Dad?" she asked.

"The houses are on stilts to catch the breeze during the hot season," he replied. He pointed toward the shore. "There's Jenna," he said happily. "I can't wait till you two meet her."

A pretty, small dark-haired woman stood on one of the docks waving and smiling. She was wearing white shorts, a bright yellow T-shirt, and sandals. She waved even harder when she saw them.

The ferry pulled around and edged its way up to the dock. The crew members jumped down and tied the ferry securely. Led by the man in the blue and red T-shirt, the men who had been playing cards pushed their way ahead of everyone and got off first. Then the other passengers got off.

Steve Richards stepped onto the dock. The twins hesitated and then followed.

Jenna rushed over to greet them. "I'm so glad you're finally here," she said. "Everything is ready. I want you to have a great time, so be sure to speak up and ask for anything you want."

"Have you got a TV?" Mike asked quickly.

"No, I'm afraid not," Jenna replied.

"Aren't we going to drive?" Mike asked.

"There are no cars here, Mike," Jenna answered. "There are a few golf carts, but everything is so close everyone just walks."

Mike looked at Maddie and whispered, "No TV and no cars. What kind of a place is this anyway?"

CHAPTER
4

Jenna was right. It was only a short walk through the town to the house. As they passed the shops and homes, people waved and said hello.

"This is a really friendly place," Jenna said enthusiastically. "I think you're going to like it."

Maddie and Mike shot looks at each other but said nothing.

"There it is," their father said. The house was on the Caribbean side of the caye. Large palms stood around it, casting a cooling shade. Lush plants with colorful flowers decorated the yard. The wood house, which was painted a bright pink, was built on stilts. A wide stairway led up to its entrance.

As they both stepped into the house, the first things they noticed were the huge windows and the beautiful view of the sea. This side of the island was also lined with docks and a number of small boats were moored in the water beyond. About a mile offshore they could see waves breaking gently on the barrier reef. Beyond the reef they could see a few more islands, but mostly the view was clear blue water.

"You each have your own room," Jenna said, leading the twins to a deck outside. Their rooms shared the same deck and were next to each other, overlooking the sea.

"My family can't wait to meet you and show you around." Jenna said. "As soon as you're ready, come out on the deck and we'll have something to eat. You must be starving."

When she had finished unpacking, Maddie stepped out of her room onto the deck. Mike appeared at almost exactly the same moment. They often did things like that, moving at the same time, saying the same things. Some people thought being twins must be wonderful, but sometimes they both felt they needed a little space. Mike had found his particular interest in sports. He was on the swim team and played baseball in the summer.

Maddie had her collections. She had stamps from around the world and her father always sent her more stamps from everywhere he visited. Maddie enjoyed swimming, too, but she was more interested in seeing what was underwater. She had a tropical fish tank at home. Both she and her brother had snorkeled in a swimming pool, but this was the first time they had a chance to really see some fish in the wild. She hoped they wouldn't run into anything dangerous.

"Come on over and have a snack," their father called from a large deck on one end of the house. Jenna had put out a tray of sandwiches and sodas.

• • •

They had just sat down to eat when they heard someone shouting from down below. A dark blue speedboat was pulling up to their dock. A boy about the twins' age, with dark brown skin and light brown eyes, was steering the boat. A large man, who looked like a bigger version of the teen, stood in the front. He jumped onto the dock as they pulled up and tied the boat securely.

"It's Jim Shaw and Brandon," Jenna said. "Jim and his son are our neighbors."

"You won't believe what we found!" Jim Shaw shouted as he came up the stairs to the deck. He was wearing an olive green swimsuit and a khaki shirt with a patch on the shoulder that said *Ranger*. His son came right behind him. He was also wearing a swimsuit and a faded blue T-shirt with tropical fish on it. Both of them looked very upset.

"What's going on?" Steve Richards asked.

"We were out on the reef snorkeling," Jim said, catching his breath. "We were looking for more of those fish that have been acting so strange, trying to get some samples. Brandon had just caught one and was putting it in a bucket on the boat when he saw it."

Brandon smiled shyly at the twins. "She was only a few feet from the boat."

"What was?" Jenna asked.

"The manatee," Jim almost shouted. "She was just wallowing in the water. She was so weak she was barely swimming at all. I thought some jerk in a speedboat had run her over and left her for dead. I could hear her struggling for breath."

"We took her to Doc Hastings," Brandon added.

"And that was no easy task, I can tell you," Jim continued. "She is almost as big as the boat."

"We tied her to the side of the boat and dragged her along," Brandon said.

"Doc looked her over and couldn't find a mark on her," Jim said. "He put her in one of his pens."

"Doc's not really a doctor," Jenna said quickly to the twins, "but he has treated manatees before and knows more about them than anyone on the whole island."

"Doc said this is the fourth sick manatee he's

seen this week," Jim continued. "This female is the worst case so far. She's so sick she might die."

"Maybe it's the one we saw, Dad," Maddie said.

"No, Maddie," her father replied. "That was on the other side of the caye. But that one was acting very peculiar, too."

"You saw a manatee from the ferry?" Jim asked.

"Yes," Maddie and Mike replied in unison.

"That's very odd," Jim said. "Very odd."

"What does Doc think made it sick?" The twins' asked.

Jim shook his head. "He doesn't know. But it might be the same thing that's making those fish act so strangely."

CHAPTER
5

Steve Richards looked around. "I'm sorry," he said, "these are my children, Maddie and Mike. They're down here for a visit." He turned to the twins. "This is Jim Shaw and his son, Brandon."

Brandon smiled broadly and put out his hand. "I'm glad to meet you. You want to go see the manatee we saved at Doc's?"

"Sure," both twins said, then looked questioningly at their dad.

"It's late," their father said, "but okay."

Brandon's father added, "Just stay for a little while. You can do things together tomorrow."

"Try to be back by sunset," Jenna said. "We have a special dinner planned."

"Come on," Brandon said. He led them down

the stairs and along the shore. There was only a narrow strip of sand, almost no beach at all. "My house is right over there," Brandon said, pointing to another house on stilts next door to their father's.

They turned and walked along a narrow sandy lane between the houses. "Is this supposed to be a road?" Mike asked.

"It's about all we need," Brandon replied. "There aren't any cars. When I visited New York, I saw all the cars I wanted to. Plus the air was hard to breathe."

"You've been to New York?" Maddie asked, sounding surprised.

"Sure. My dad went up there to attend an environmental meeting at the United Nations. He was representing the Belize National Parks. He's a Chief Ranger," he said proudly. Then Brandon turned toward the water. "It's this way."

Ahead of them was a pier that looked much bigger and more solid than the ones they had seen before. Attached to it was a series of pens formed by hanging nets underwater from floating logs, with planks to walk on and platforms to view the animals. The pens looked like a jigsaw puzzle of logs and platforms. Out near the last pen, a huge man with white hair that stuck out from under a green cap knelt, staring into the water.

"Hey, Doc," Brandon called.

The large man waved, but he didn't get up.

Stepping carefully, Brandon led the way through the maze of planks to where Doc was. As they approached they could see that he was watching a manatee in the pen. The manatee was barely moving, but it came to the surface and took a breath as they came nearer.

"How's she doing?" Brandon asked.

Doc sighed. "She seems a little livelier. I gave her a shot of vitamins. I don't think there's anything else we can do."

Maddie and Mike knelt down and looked closely at the manatee. It lay on its back just below the surface of the water. They could see its small front flippers and its large round tail.

"This is Maddie and Mike," Brandon said. "They're visiting their father, Mr. Steve Richards."

"Ah, yes," Doc said. "Your father told me you'd be coming down here. Welcome to Caye Caulker, although you've come at a bad time."

Mike and Maddie said together. "Bad time?"

"Yes," Doc responded. "Something is wrong with the creatures in the sea. We may have to close the reef until we can figure out what it is."

"Can't you do anything to help this poor manatee?" Brandon asked.

"I guess all we can do is let it alone," Doc said, getting slowly to his feet. "The tide is running pretty good. Clean ocean water might help," he said as he led them toward the shore. The wooden dock shifted under his weight and water flowed over the planks.

"Can I offer you something to drink?" Doc Hastings asked. "I've got soda in the cooler."

"No, thanks, Doc," Brandon replied. "We all have to be getting back for dinner."

"We saw another manatee," Maddie said. "It was acting strange, too . . . at least that's what Dad said."

Doc seemed interested. "Where was it?" he asked.

Mike and Maddie explained what they had seen on the ferry and how the manatee had stared at them as they passed.

"Manatees don't usually go out that far," Doc remarked.

"That's what Dad said," Maddie replied.

"He said that in the old days sailors thought manatees were mermaids," Mike added.

"That's true," Doc said, "or so some people think. There used to be a lot more of them in the Caribbean and off the coast of Florida. Now there are only a few thousand left in the whole world.

A few summers ago one of them swam all the way up the coast from Florida past New York to Rhode Island. The newspapers called it 'Chessie,' after the Chesapeake Bay, where he was first seen. He surprised a lot of people."

"Did he make it back?" Mike asked.

"Yes, he did. He was seen back in Florida a few weeks later." Doc paused. "Manatees don't have any natural enemies, except humans. And that's mostly by accident. High-powered speedboats can run into them, sometimes without even knowing it. A spinning propeller can cut up a manatee pretty badly."

"Dad told us," Maddie said with a shudder.

"People on the cayes have formed a committee to watch what is happening," Brandon said. "We rescue injured animals and bring them to Doc."

Doc nodded. "But the one you brought me today wasn't hit by a boat. That's what I see most of the time. This is a real puzzle. I don't know what is making her sick. It may be pollution or something she ate, but this is the fourth manatee like this I've seen this week."

"Four?" Mike asked.

"Yup," Doc replied. "The other three are in that large pen farther out on the dock. They seem to be getting better, but very slowly. I'll let 'em go as soon as they are well, but I'd sure like to know what is making them sick." He shifted his hat and looked out toward the reef sadly. "Something horrible is happening out there, and I don't know what it is."

CHAPTER
6

The town was dark when they went to dinner. Dad and Jenna took them to a restaurant near the north end of the caye. They didn't need to dress up like they did when they went to restaurants back home in the city. The restaurant was built overlooking a narrow channel that divided the caye in half.

"It's called the 'cut,'" Dad explained. "The big hurricane of 1961 washed out the channel. A lot of people swim there now, but sometimes the current is a little swift."

Maddie and Mike both liked the restaurant, but for very different reasons. Maddie like it because it was decorated with fishing nets and everything was made from seashells, even the lamps. Mike thought that the restaurant was cool because there were swords and pistols hanging on the walls and a pirate flag with a skull and crossbones hanging from the ceiling. When Jenna introduced the twins to the owner, he seemed genuinely happy to meet them and took them all to their table.

"There used to be lots of pirates in this area," Jenna told them. "Mostly they were British ships raiding Spanish treasure ships coming from the silver mines in Mexico and Panama. Men like Sir Francis Drake and Blackbeard also raided the Spanish settlements along the coast."

"We read about Drake in class," Maddie said. "Some kids got to go to Switzerland because they solved the mystery of Drake's treasure."

"I remember that," Mike said.

"Drake didn't come to Belize, as far as we know," Jenna continued, "but there are stories about pirate treasure on almost all the cayes and tales of shipwrecks on the reef. Caye Caulker is supposed to have been named by pirates. They called a wild coco plum 'corker.' This caye was covered with them, and the pirates used them for food. At least that's how the story goes."

"How do you know all that stuff?" Mike asked.

"My family has been here for generations," Jenna replied. "I grew up in Belize City and went to school in England. I lived with my relatives there, but I decided I liked the sunshine and sand a lot more than the cold and rain in London. So, I came back. But I travel a lot, like your father." She smiled at Steve Richards and squeezed his hand.

Maddie shot a look at Mike, but Dad and Jenna didn't seem to notice. They were still smiling at each other.

The restaurant owner came over to take their orders. Mike and Maddie both ordered hamburgers. The owner wanted to put his special sauce on their burgers, but Jenna asked for it on the side.

"A few coins and some relics have been found by divers near the cayes," their father said, "but no big treasure. Still, people are looking all the time."

"A lot of settlers from England and Scotland came here," Jenna added, "just like my family. The Spanish kept trying to claim the land, but finally they were beaten by Baymen from Belize in a battle off St. George's Caye, just south of here."

"We passed it on the ferry," Dad said to Maddie and Mike.

"We drove the Spaniards off on September 10, 1798," Jenna continued. "September 10th is like your Fourth of July. We call it National Day."

The owner brought their food and placed it in front of them. Jenna was having fish with rice and beans, and their father was having fried lobster. The owner placed large hamburgers with potato chips in front of each of the twins and a large bowl of red sauce between them. The sauce looked like catsup, but when Mike tasted it, it was so hot it made him choke. Maddie and Jenna laughed when he gulped down a whole glass of water.

"You can get a hamburger just about anywhere around here, Mike," Jenna told him, "but you have to watch out for what they put on it. Your father once had a hamburger with bananas on it."

After dinner they walked home. The twins lagged behind their father and Jenna. They could hear them talking and laughing.

"Do you think she made all that stuff up?" Maddie asked Mike as they walked along.

"No," Mike said. "Why would she do that?"

"I don't know. I'm just not sure I trust her. What do you think of her?"

"I kinda like her. She's funny, and Dad is sure smiling a lot."

"But Jenna's really different from Mom," Maddie said.

Mike thought for a moment. "Yeah," he said. "She's short and she has dark hair. Mom is tall and has blonde hair—like we do."

"No," Maddie responded. "That's not what I mean. She's so outgoing and . . . too friendly . . . or something. Mom is serious and brainy . . . like a lawyer . . . ."

"She *is* a lawyer, Maddie," Mike said, starting to sound a little impatient.

A rowdy group of men came toward them out of the darkness, laughing and talking loudly. The twins had to move to the side of the narrow road as the men pushed past them. Maddie thought she recognized the man who had been wearing the blue and red shirt on the ferry.

"Are you two okay?" their father asked when the twins caught up with them.

"That was pretty rude," Jenna remarked. "They're not from this caye."

When they reached their house, Jenna said goodnight by giving each of them a kiss on the cheek. Then she went off to her house.

"I'm bushed," Dad said once they were inside. "You can find your way to your rooms, can't you?"

Maddie and Mike nodded yes. Their father went to his room at the front of the house and the twins went out to the dark deck that ran alongside their rooms.

"Hey!" somebody whispered from the shadows.

"What!" they both said, startled.

"It's me. Brandon." Brandon Shaw stepped into the light. "I brought you some of the stuff my Dad has collected about the manatees." He handed them a folder filled with papers. "It's pretty scary."

"Come on in, Brandon," Mike said, pointing toward his room.

"Can't," Brandon replied. "I promised my folks I'd come right back. You can give me back that stuff tomorrow." He turned and climbed over the railing of the deck and dropped to the sand. As the twins watched, he waved and disappeared into the dark.

"Wow!" Mike exclaimed later. "Look at all this stuff." The file was filled with newspaper articles and photos of injured manatees.

Both twins looked and read for a few moments in silence. "This is terrible," Maddie finally said. "All those boats crashing into the poor manatees."

Mike nodded grimly. "In a few years there won't be any manatees left."

"We should talk to Brandon about what we can do to help," Maddie continued.

"Tomorrow, Maddie," Mike said. "I'm exhausted."

There was a light breeze and ceiling fans in each bedroom, but they both tossed and turned in the heat, thinking about the injured manatees and everything they had seen. Eventually, the noise of the ocean waves lulled them to sleep.

Maddie started to dream about manatees and how cute their wrinkled snouts were. The manatees pirouetted in the water and splashed her with their large round tails. She couldn't wait to go swimming with them. Then a huge boat came roaring past.

Maddie's eyes snapped open. Was she dreaming or did she just hear a boat?

"What's that?" she heard Mike say from the next room.

Maddie got up quickly and went out on the deck. Mike was already there, peering into the night. The roar of a speedboat filled the air, drowning out all other sounds.

"There it is!" Mike said. Through the palm trees along the shore they caught sight of a gleaming white speedboat. It was racing out toward the reef, leaving a trail of white water behind it. Far ahead of it they could see bright lights and dark shapes bobbing in the water. The speedboat headed straight toward the lights and disappeared into the darkness.

Then in an instant the distant lights went out!

CHAPTER
7

"Is that you?" a voice in the darkness whispered.

"Yeah, it's me," Mike answered.

"And me, too." Maddie giggled. "Who else would it be?"

Brandon appeared on the deck of his house next door. "Did you see that boat?"

"See it?" Mike replied. "It made so much noise it shook me out of bed."

"Was it a big white speedboat?" Brandon asked.

"Yeah," both twins answered.

"Running without lights?"

"Yeah."

"It's done that before."

"Gone racing past here in the middle of the night, you mean?" Maddie asked.

"Toward all those lights we saw?" Mike added.

"What lights?" Brandon asked.

"There were a bunch of lights and stuff out there," Mike said, pointing toward the ocean, "way far out. They were really bright and then they went out."

"Yeah," Maddie chimed in. "There were lots of shapes moving around in the light. And then they disappeared."

Brandon thought for a minute. "I've seen that speedboat twice in the last week. It always heads out toward the reef and disappears. But I've never seen any lights out there."

"They were there tonight," Mike declared.

"There's an automatic lighthouse out there," Brandon replied, "but you can't see it very well from here. The Turneffe Islands are in the way. There's nothing else out there that I know of. Lighthouse Reef is deserted, too."

"There was something out there tonight," Maddie insisted. "We both saw it."

"Well, whatever it was, it wasn't there this afternoon," Brandon replied, pointing toward where the twins had seen the bobbing lights. "That's where my dad and I were snorkeling. It's right near the edge of the barrier reef. Nobody's supposed to be out there at night. It's way too dangerous."

"Maybe it's pirates," Mike suggested.

"Maybe you'd like to take a look with me," Brandon responded.

"Awesome!" Mike said. "I'll get dressed."

Brandon laughed. "Not now, Dude. We'll go out tomorrow when it's light. You guys meet me at the dock after breakfast."

CHAPTER
8

Their father was standing in front of the stove cooking eggs when the twins came in. "You still like them scrambled?" he asked.

"Definitely!" Mike exclaimed.

"Did you hear that speedboat last night, Dad?" Maddie asked.

"Nope," he replied, lifting the frying pan off the stove and bringing it over to the kitchen table. "Boats go by here all the time, though, so I probably wouldn't notice." He looked at his watch.

"We saw it," Mike said.

"It headed out toward some lights in the distance," Maddie added.

"Then the lights disappeared," Mike finished.

"I've got to get going," their father said. "I have

to check in with the project. Then we're going to meet Jenna and run some last-minute errands for the wedding."

"But, Dad," Mike said between forkfuls of scrambled eggs. "Isn't that light a little strange?"

"You probably just saw the automatic light out on Lighthouse Reef. It's solar powered and comes on every night to warn boats away from the reef. You mistook it for something else. There's nothing else out there except the Turneffe Islands, and nobody lives on them."

Maddie shook her head. "It was too bright for that."

"Can we talk about it later?" Dad asked. "It's starting to get crazy with all the wedding plans. Plus I've got a deadline to meet on the survey I'm doing. Jenna and some of her family are due here any minute to meet you two."

There was a knock at the front door. "Right on cue," he said as he went to open the door.

Maddie and Mike looked at each other nervously. They weren't exactly thrilled to be meeting Jenna's relatives.

A moment later their dad returned with Jenna and an older couple. She introduced her mother and father to the twins. "We're going on the ferry to Belize City to pick up some things," Jenna said. "You kids are welcome to come along."

Maddie and Mike told her that they wanted to hang out with Brandon. Their dad seemed disappointed, but Jenna and her mother said it was good for them to spend time with someone their own age.

"Just remember to be back for a barbecue at six o'clock," Jenna said. "My brother and some friends are coming over." She looked at her watch. "Oh, my gosh!" she exclaimed. "We've got to hurry or we'll miss the ferry."

"And I've got to get to the office. I have to finish up my report or there won't be any wedding," the twins' dad said.

Jenna put her hands on her hips. "You're not getting out of it that easily," she said, pretending to threaten him.

This time it was Mike who looked at Maddie. They quickly said their good-byes, grabbed their snorkling equipment, and shot out of the house.

Brandon was waiting for them on the dock below his father's house. He waved and smiled as they approached and started to untie the lines that held his small rubber dinghy to the dock. It was bright green and yellow, and it had a small outboard motor mounted on its stern.

"Sorry we're late," Maddie said. "There's a lot of confusion at Dad's house with getting ready for the wedding and all."

"No problem," Brandon said.

"Let's get going," Mike said, putting his mask and fins into the dinghy.

Maddie looked at the rubber boat doubtfully. "Are you sure this is safe?" she asked.

"Definitely," Brandon replied. "I use it all the time."

The water was smooth, except for a gentle swell, and very clear. They could see white sand and large rocks on the bottom passing below as Brandon guided the dinghy toward the reef.

"I'm going to take you to one of my favorite diving spots," Brandon said over the sound of the outboard motor. "It's out near Lighthouse Reef. Maybe we can see about those lights."

"How far is it?" Mike asked.

"Not too far," Brandon replied. "There are lots of places we could go on the reef, but I like to spend as much time as I can in the water, not in my boat. Besides, we're going where Dad and I found that sick manatee."

"You mean there might be more manatees out there?" Maddie asked.

"Maybe. Dad said it's the first time he's ever seen one out this far, but manatees usually travel in groups."

"I hope we'll find one," Maddie said excitedly.

"We might," Brandon responded, "but the reef's a big place. If they've come out this far, they could be anywhere."

A short while later Brandon slowed the boat. He shut down the outboard motor and threw the anchor overboard. The rubber boat drifted for a moment and then the anchor caught on the bottom, holding it fast.

"You guys stay with me," Brandon said. "If we get separated, come back to the boat. The water's pretty flat today so you shouldn't have any trouble finding it."

As Maddie and Mike put on their fins and adjusted their masks and snorkels, Brandon rolled over the side into the water. "C'mon!" he said. "No time to waste."

Mike stood up and jumped over the side with a great splash, leaving Maddie rocking madly in the dinghy as it swung on its anchor line. Water sloshed over the sides of the boat.

Mike came up sputtering, with his mask and snorkel twisted around to the side of his head. Brandon pushed his mask up to his forehead and laughed loudly, but Maddie was scared as she held on to the rocking boat.

"Done much snorkeling, Dudes?" Brandon asked the twins mockingly.

"We've done a little," Maddie admitted, "but only in the swimming pool and at the lake at summer camp."

"And in the bathtub," Mike said, laughing. He was holding on to the bobbing dinghy with one hand and straightening his mask with the other.

"Hold on to your mask and jump in backward, Maddie," Brandon advised. "That'll keep it from riding up like Mike's."

Maddie jumped into the ocean the way Brandon suggested and her mask stayed in place. The water was warm and felt great.

"Follow me," Brandon said once he was sure they all had their equipment ready. He kicked his fins and set off for the reef.

Seeing underwater was like discovering a new world. The bottom looked like it was only a few feet away, and it was covered with colorful coral and strands of seaweed waving in the gentle current. There was a forest of huge orange fan-shaped corals and thickets of white corals shaped like the horns of a deer. Below them were darker shapes, mounds and crevices of brown and green corals, and huge round shapes marked with intricate patterns of furrows and ridges.

Brandon stopped and lifted his head out of the water and removed his snorkel. "That's brain coral down there," he said to the twins.

"It looks like something from outer space," Mike responded, after taking off his snorkel.

"The stuff that looks like tree branches is staghorn coral," Brandon continued.

"Let's keep going," Maddie said, holding her snorkel in her hand.

Brandon led the way.

As their eyes became accustomed to what they were seeing, they began to notice other things, like bright shapes darting in and out of the coral. There were fish of all shapes and colors. A large green and red fish, which looked like a parrot, was nibbling on the coral with its sharp beak. Around it were smaller bright neon blue and yellow fish. Then they saw a stately golden angelfish go by. Below, a school of bright orange fish nestled together in a small dark cave at the bottom of the reef. The reef was teeming with life!

Brandon lifted his head out of the water and removed his snorkel. Mike and Maddie surfaced right beside him. "I'll show you a cleaning station," Brandon said. "It's weird, but big fish let little ones clean their scales. The little fish eat parasites and algae. They're called cleaning wrasse. C'mon."

They swam toward a formation of rocks on the reef. At first it looked like all the other rocks to

Maddie and Mike, but then they noticed a large brown fish floating in the shadows. Several small bright blue and red fish hovered around the large one, searching its scales and touching them with their mouths. The large fish stayed put, letting the smaller ones do their work. One small fish even disappeared into the larger fish's mouth. It reappeared a moment later and continued working.

Brandon signaled them to surface again.

"Whoa!" Mike said when he got the snorkel out of his mouth. "I thought that little fish was a goner when it went inside the big one's mouth."

Brandon laughed. "Nope. They never eat cleaning wrasses. Sometimes I think the bigger fish like being cleaned."

"What's that other fish I saw?" Maddie asked. "The one off to the side? It had orange and white stripes and looked like it was sitting on a flower?"

"That's not a flower, Maddie," Brandon replied. "It's a sea anemone. They look beautiful, but they have poison stingers that can be pretty painful if you touch them. They use the poison in their stingers to paralyze fish and, then, eat them. But clown fish have figured out how to live inside anemones without getting stung. The anemone protects the clown fish and it keeps the anemone clean."

With Brandon in the lead, they turned and swam

along the edge of the reef. A large school of long, thin silver-colored fish caught their attention. They looked like thin pencils as they swam along, just below the surface of the ocean. They came close to the teens, but kept out of their reach.

As the teens swung around in the water to follow the silver fish, they noticed two large dark shapes in the distance. They recognized them in an instant: manatees!

Brandon came to the surface. "Do you see them?" he asked excitedly.

Both twins answered, "Yes."

"Let's go over there to get a closer look, but don't get too close. We don't want to scare them. I want to see if we can figure out what they're doing out this far."

The three swam slowly toward the manatees. Although they were huge, underwater the manatees moved in a graceful ballet. The pair swam side by side and then slowly went over and under each other, trading places. The manatees nuzzled the bottom occasionally, but they didn't seem to find anything interesting. Their great round tails moved smoothly up and down, slowly carrying them across the reef. They rose occasionally to the surface to get a breath of air.

Brandon gestured to the twins to come up to the

surface again. "These guys aren't sick like the other one," he said, "but I still don't see why they are out this far."

When the teens looked back underwater at the manatees, they had changed position. The manatees were hovering nose-to-nose. Then they slowly swam upward until their heads were out of the water and they seemed to embrace each other like two dancers waltzing.

Mike laughed into his snorkel and then began to choke. He bobbed to the surface with Maddie right behind.

"Did you ever see anything so silly looking," Mike said as he caught his breath.

"But they're so cute," Maddie protested. "They were dancing!"

"But they look so clumsy," Mike said.

"No, they don't. You're just being mean," Maddie replied.

"Where's Brandon?" Mike asked. He looked around. The boat was only a short distance away.

"I don't know," Maddie replied, looking in all directions, "but we'd better find him."

They pulled down their masks and looked underwater. But Brandon was nowhere to be seen. The manatees were gone, too.

"*Ook! Ook!*" Maddie heard Mike yelling through his snorkel. He pulled on her leg.

Maddie slapped his hand away. "Stop fooling around," she tried to tell him, but her snorkel was in the way.

Then something caught Maddie's eye. She reached out and grabbed Mike's arm and pointed. A dark shape loomed out of the distance and swept over the coral toward them. It was shaped like a bat and very black.

Mike pulled his snorkel out of his mouth. "That's what I was trying to show you!" he shouted. "It's a stingray!"

It looked like a stingray. Both the twins had seen stingrays in the aquarium at home. But this one was bigger—much bigger. It was slowly flapping its huge wings, and it was headed right toward them!

Maddie and Mike turned toward the boat and began swimming as fast as they could. Their fins pumped against the water, turning it to white foam.

Maddie was just behind Mike when her mask slipped down over her face. Salt water stung her eyes. She tried to fix her mask, but she had to stop swimming. Mike splashed away, heading for the boat.

As Maddie pulled her mask back into place,

she glanced back. The dark shape was moving ever so slowly, but it was much closer. She could see its gaping mouth and its long, whip-like tail. The monster was huge!

CHAPTER
9

Mike swam ahead of Maddie, his arms and legs flailing. The boat was only a few strokes away. He clambered over the side and fell into the bottom of the rubber boat. He tore off his mask and leaned over the side to help Maddie.

Maddie was moving as fast as she could, but Mike could see that the black shape just below the surface of the water was gaining on her. "Hurry, Maddie," he shouted. "Hurry!"

Maddie's hand touched the side of the boat. The black creature was right behind. Maddie's other hand came up. Mike grabbed it and pulled. He struggled and then Maddie spilled into the boat. The black creature swept by, passing under the boat.

"Look!" Mike shouted. "It's bigger than the boat."

And it was. The width of its great black wings was larger than the length of Brandon's dinghy.

Maddie was breathing hard. "Do you think it will try to get us?" she said between gasps.

"I don't know," Mike replied. "Maybe . . ."

But the great ray kept on going in the same direction, swimming smoothly away from the boat.

"Hey," a voice said from behind them.

The twins spun around. It was Brandon. "Where'd you guys go?"

"That black fish tried to get us," Maddie blurted out.

"It was as big as the boat," Mike added. "It wanted to eat us."

Brandon pulled himself into the boat and laid his mask and snorkel in the bottom. "No, it didn't," he said calmly.

"It was a giant stingray," Mike insisted, "and it was going to sting us."

"It was a giant ray all right," Brandon replied, but it wasn't a stingray. It was a giant manta. Mantas don't have stingers."

"But I saw its mouth," Maddie said. "It was coming right for me."

Brandon laughed. "As big as they are, mantas eat only the tiniest things, the plankton and other microscopic animals in the sea. That big mouth is a scoop that takes in huge amounts of water so they can filter out the plankton."

"You mean it wasn't after us?" Mike asked. He seemed disappointed.

Brandon shook his head. "No, it was just passing over the reef looking for its tiny dinner. It's here all the time. Some divers even hitch rides on the backs of mantas."

Mike looked at Maddie and smiled with relief. Then they both blushed and laughed a little with embarrassment.

"It's more likely to tip the boat over by accident than it is to attack us in the water," Brandon continued.

Maddie quickly looked around at the water. "Oh," she said sarcastically, "that makes me feel *much* better."

They dove in several other places on the reef and each time the twins were struck by how beautiful it was underwater. But they both kept a wary eye out for any other large black fish that might come near them. Finally the wind came up and they decided to head back to Caye Caulker.

It was late in the afternoon when they arrived at Brandon's dock. They tied up the boat and headed for their houses.

As Maddie and Mike approached their father's

house they could see that someone had done a lot of work decorating for the party. There were several tables set up on the deck, covered with white tablecloths and big bunches of brightly colored flowers. Paper streamers and lanterns were hung from the roof. More flowers sat in clay pots along the edge of the deck.

Jenna waved as they approached. "Hello," she said. "You both look as though you could use a shower and some clean clothes."

Mike and Maddie had to agree. Their hair was tangled and wild from swimming, and their arms and legs were coated with salt from the ocean water.

"Go on in and clean up for the party," Jenna said. "We've got some time before the guests arrive, and I want to hear all about what you saw."

There was the deep rumbling sound of an engine coming from the ocean. Mike and Maddie looked, but they couldn't see where it was coming from. The palm trees along the shore blocked their view.

Jenna shielded her eyes with one hand. "There he is," she said over the roar.

A large white speedboat came into sight and landed at the dock below the house. A man shut down the engine and jumped onto the dock.

"It's the boat from last night!" the twins said at almost the same time.

Jenna didn't seem to hear them. "Come on down," she said, grabbing their hands, "and meet my brother Tim."

CHAPTER
10

"Did you see the white speedboat?" Maddie asked Brandon the first chance she got at the party.

Brandon and his father had arrived late and there had been too much confusion to talk before this. But now the guests had finished eating and were sitting around joking and sharing stories. A small band with guitars and a steel drum played, and a few couples danced under the brightly colored lanterns that hung from wires strung above the deck. Paper streamers added to the festive look of the house, along with the beautiful bunches of tropical flowers Jenna had arranged on each table.

Brandon and the twins sat at a small table near the edge of the deck, overlooking the shore below. Brandon's parents were sitting at another table with the twins' father and Jenna and Doc Hastings.

Brandon had been teasing the twins all night over their encounter with the manta. "There's nothing it could do to you except flap you to death with its humongous wings," he said, laughing.

Finally Mike's face flushed with embarrassment and he started to say something, but Maddie spoke first. "Okay, okay, you've made us feel like total dorks. Maybe if you'd told us *before* we saw the manta we would have known better."

Brandon stopped smiling. "You're right," he said seriously after a moment. "I should have warned you. Sorry."

Mike, whose anger always disappeared as fast as it rose, looked toward the dock. "Did you see Jenna's brother arrive?"

"No," Brandon replied.

"He came in that boat." Mike pointed toward the white speedboat. "The one tied up there."

"It looks like the one we saw last night," Maddie added.

Brandon got up from the table and stood by the railing of the deck where he could see better. The twins joined him. "Yeah," he said as he peered at the boat. "It sure looks like the one I saw, too."

"Whata ya lookin' at, kid?" a gruff voice asked from behind them.

It was Jenna's brother, Tim. Although the twins had met him briefly when he arrived, this was the first time they had really gotten a good look at him. He was very tall and thin. He wore his long brown hair in a ponytail. He hunched his shoulders as he looked down at them, giving his body a slightly curved shape that somehow seemed threatening. He wore a short-sleeved shirt with a bright tropical pattern of blues and oranges. He was deeply tanned from the sun.

"You admiring my boat?" Tim asked. He smiled, but his eyes didn't smile. They were cold and black.

"Uh, yes," Maddie managed to answer.

"How fast is it?" Mike asked.

"Plenty fast," Tim answered. "It'll outrun just about any boat around here."

"How come you need such a fast boat around here?" Maddie asked.

Tim looked at her sharply. "I just do, that's all." He smiled his cold grin again.

"If you go too fast, aren't you likely to hit something?" Brandon asked.

Tim turned toward him. "Like what?"

"Like a manatee, maybe," Maddie chimed in nervously.

"No way," Tim said.

"You do much running at night?" Brandon asked.

Tim's eyes narrowed. "Can't say I do," he said evasively.

"Without lights?" Brandon added.

"For kids who are supposed to be here for a wedding," Jenna's brother said menacingly, "you're asking an awful lot of snoopy questions. You should mind your own business!" He turned and stalked away.

"What a creep," Mike said.

"Maybe we should tell Dad," Maddie ventured.

"Tell him what?" Mike asked. "That Jenna's brother is a creep?"

"Besides," Maddie said, "we don't want to spoil Dad's wedding. This is supposed to be a happy time."

"I've got a better idea," Brandon said. "Let's keep watch tonight and see if he goes by again. If he does, then we can tell both our dads."

CHAPTER
11

"Can you see anything?" Mike whispered, leaning out to look at the dark ocean. They were crowded into a small storage shed on the dock in front of Brandon's house.

"No," Brandon replied, "but this is about the time of night the boat usually comes by."

A light breeze made the palm trees nearby rustle. Small clouds drifted past the pale crescent moon.

"Move over," Maddie said irritably to Mike. "You're standing on my foot."

"Shhh!" Mike responded, turning toward her.

"What's that?" Brandon asked.

There was a distant roar of a powerful motor.

"It must be him!" Maddie said as the roar grew louder.

A moment later they could see the white speed-boat moving slowly down the coast toward them, its engine idling.

"It's him!" Maddie said as the boat came closer.

Even in the dim light of the moon they could see that it was Tim, Jenna's brother, steering the boat.

"Yeah," Brandon agreed. "It's him all right."

Tim seemed to look back in their direction. Then the white boat suddenly thundered into action, swiftly picking up speed as its engine roared. It headed past the dock where the three were hiding and then turned away, racing out toward the reef, its white wake spreading behind it.

"Come on!" Brandon said. He led the way down the dock to where his dinghy was tied. "Get in," he said.

Mike stepped down into the rubber boat, but Maddie held back. "What are we doing?" she asked.

"We're going to follow him out and see where he's going," Brandon replied.

"But it's dark," Maddie said. "How will we ever find him?"

"We'll never catch him in this," Mike added.

Brandon rolled his eyes. "We don't need to catch him. I just want to see where he's going. Then we'll *really* have something to tell our dads."

"Okay," Maddie said doubtfully as she climbed

into the dinghy. Brandon pulled the cord to start the outboard motor and Mike cast off. Brandon turned the dinghy in the direction the white speedboat had taken.

Maddie and Mike began to regret being on the dinghy as soon as they drew away from Caye Caulker. The ocean was smooth, except for small swells kicked up by the light breeze, but it seemed very dark and empty as the lights of the caye faded behind them.

Brandon kept the boat steady, moving ahead. The small outboard motor sputtered occasionally, but it kept running.

Maddie looked down at the water and wondered what creatures lurked beneath them. The rubber bottom of the boat didn't seem like much protection. Several long silver fish torpedoed past the boat. "What's that?" she asked. Her voice was louder than she expected, even with the sound of the outboard.

Brandon looked unconcerned. "Just tarpon or maybe barracuda. They hunt at night."

Mike hesitated for a moment. Then he asked, "Don't barracuda attack people?"

Brandon kept staring straight ahead. "Not that I know of," he said.

Maddie decided to keep her eyes on where they were going. She heard a small splash but ignored it.

Then there was a large splash next to the dinghy. Mike jumped back and shouted, "Whoa!" as water splashed over him.

Brandon swiftly turned the boat in a circle and shut down the engine.

"What is it?" Maddie asked urgently.

Brandon looked around. "I don't know," he said slowly, "but it seems to be gone."

"No, it's not," Mike said, his voice full of fear.

A huge black shape surfaced a few feet from the rubber boat.

"It's a shark!" Maddie exclaimed.

"No . . . ," Brandon said uncertainly. He fumbled for something in the bottom of the boat.

The black shape turned and headed for the boat.

"Let's get out of here," Mike urged.

"Maybe it's a manatee," Brandon said as he pulled a flashlight out and shined it toward the black beast.

The flashlight revealed only a shiny black mound bobbing in the water, but as Brandon moved the light around, it became clear that the black creature was huge, bigger than the dinghy.

"What is it?" Maddie shouted, barely controlling her terror.

The creature shifted in the water and there was a flash of white on its underside.

"It's the manta," Brandon said at last. "It won't hurt us."

"You told us that mantas tip over boats," Mike complained.

"I was just trying to scare you."

The manta feebly waved its huge black fins, barely keeping itself from being swept along by the tide. It wobbled in the water, moving uncertainly from side to side. It seemed to be struggling just to keep swimming.

"Something's wrong," Brandon declared. "It's not swimming right."

The manta flopped sideways, one of its winglike fins coming completely out of the water. For a moment it looked like it was going to flip over on its back, but it tottered and turned upright with a great splash. Then it moved unsteadily away from the boat, weaving along the surface of the water.

"I've never seen a fish behave like that before," Brandon said. "Mantas glide through the water. That one couldn't even stay steady."

"That's what Doc Hastings said about the sick manatees," Maddie responded. "They had trouble swimming right. Maybe it's the same thing."

"Whoa!" Mike said suddenly. "Look out!"

In the moonlight they could see dark shapes moving toward them over the water. Brandon

64

quickly pulled the cord that started the motor. The motor coughed but didn't start.

"What is it?" Maddie asked tensely.

"Something's coming to get us!" Mike replied.

"No," Brandon said as he wound the pull cord on the motor. "It's the Turneffe Islands. The tide is carrying us toward a patch of mangrove. At this speed the roots could rip the bottom of the dinghy. Mike, grab an oar and try to push us off."

Mike pulled an oar from the bottom of the dinghy and kneeled in the bow, ready to push off.

The dark shapes grew larger and then loomed over them. They could make out individual mangrove shrubs looming over the water. Brandon yanked on the starter cord.

In the distance, a bright light came and swept across the water toward them!

CHAPTER
12

The motor started suddenly, pushing the boat forward. Mike fell backward into the dinghy. Brandon turned the boat hard, pulling its bow away from the mangroves and pointing them out to sea. Maddie stood up and tried to reach Mike who lay on the floor of the dinghy.

"Get down!" Brandon shouted.

The bright light swept across the ocean again, briefly illuminating the boat with a blinding white glare. Then it moved on, sweeping over the mangroves and out of sight.

"What was that?" Mike asked, climbing out of the bottom of the boat.

Brandon slowed the engine and stood up for a

moment to look around. "I don't know," he said, "but I'd sure like to find out."

"It's the same light we saw last night," Maddie said.

"Yeah," Brandon agreed, "and it sure isn't the light on Lighthouse Reef. Something really weird is going on."

"Let's see what it is," Mike said excitedly.

"Okay," Brandon replied. "We can use the mangroves for cover, as long as we're careful not to go too fast."

Keeping the dinghy in the shallows near the mangrove thicket, Brandon moved them slowly toward the source of the light. Mike and Maddie both held oars so they could push off if the dinghy bumped into anything.

"This place stinks," Maddie remarked after a few moments.

"Yeah," Mike agreed. "It smells awful—like a sewer or something."

"It's just the mangroves," Brandon replied. "Most islands around here are surrounded by mangrove forests, even small ones like the Turneffes. The mangroves hold the sand and gradually the islands get bigger. But the roots form a swamp that smells pretty foul. Hey, guys, we'd better be quiet now."

Brandon shut off the engine and moved to the middle seat in the dinghy. He took the oars from the twins and slowly rowed the boat around the small island.

The twins watched for rocks as Brandon moved the dinghy carefully in the moonlight.

"Look out!" Mike said, reaching down to push the boat away from a large pointed rock in the water. "That was close."

Brandon stopped rowing for a moment to rest, but the boat kept moving.

"Where are we going?" Maddie asked uneasily.

"The tide is carrying us," Brandon replied. "This is way easier than rowing."

As the tide carried them smoothly around the end of the small island the bright lights became visible in the distance. They seemed to flicker and bounce.

"That's what we saw," Maddie whispered.

Brandon nodded.

"But why are they moving?" Mike asked.

The dinghy floated closer and the scene became clearer. The lights were coming from spotlights on several small boats that were bobbing in front of what looked like a large flat barge. They could see people moving around on the barge, sometimes passing in front of the lights and causing them to flicker even more.

It was Mike who first noticed the other boat hidden in the shadows of the mangroves. He signaled to the others and pointed.

Maddie and Brandon looked where Mike was pointing. Even in the moonlight they could barely make out the other boat against the mangroves, it was so carefully concealed.

Someone moved on the boat. A man stood on the deck with his back to them, holding binoculars to his eyes. He was looking in the direction of the barge and the lights. He seemed to be studying the scene very carefully.

The tide was pushing the dinghy directly toward the concealed boat. Trying to be as quiet as possible, Brandon dipped the oars into the water and began rowing. The oarlocks creaked, but the man didn't seem to notice.

The dinghy slowed, but the tide kept moving it toward the other boat. They could see the man on board more clearly. He was wearing some sort of earphones connected to a cone-shaped device set on the railing of his boat. The device was pointed toward the barge with the lights.

"He's spying," Mike whispered.

"Maybe he can't hear us with those earphones on," Maddie suggested.

Brandon rowed harder, but the distance between

the boats was still closing. They were going to hit the speedboat dead on.

Maddie gasped. She recognized the man with the binoculars. It was Jenna's creepy brother Tim!

CHAPTER 13

Brandon stopped rowing and scrambled to the bow of the dinghy.

"What are you doing?" both twins exclaimed.

The dinghy moved more swiftly toward the specdboat hidden in the mangrove. They were definitely going to hit it.

Brandon grabbed the line that was tied to the bow. He searched the water for a moment and then reached out into the shallows. He grabbed a mangrove root just below the surface and quickly attached the line to it.

The tide took the dinghy forward a little farther, but then the rope stopped it short with a jerk. The current swung the dinghy around on the rope until it was facing away from the speedboat. The dinghy jerked again against the line, but the line and the root held.

"Give me a hand," Brandon whispered. Mike and Maddie helped him pull the line into the dinghy, moving it slowly away from the speedboat.

"Hold on to the root," Brandon whispered to Mike. Mike leaned over the side and grabbed it. "Hold tight," Brandon said as he untied the line.

Mike kept the dinghy in place while Brandon picked up an oar and handed it to Maddie. "We're going to push over into the mangrove," he said, picking up the other oar.

"Won't it tear the bottom?" Maddie asked.

"Not if we're careful," Brandon whispered back.

They pushed against the bottom with the oars. Mike let go of the root and the dinghy slid gently into the mangrove thicket. They all ducked as they moved under the overhanging branches. Brandon guided them into the swampy thicket until the other boat was out of sight.

"If we can't see him," Brandon said softly, "he won't see us."

There was a loud splash near the dinghy.

"Keep quiet!" Brandon ordered.

The twins looked at each other. "We didn't do anything," Mike responded.

There was another loud splash.

"Must be the tide," Brandon suggested.

"No, no," Maddie said. "Look there!"

In the shallows near the boat they could make out a gray shape floundering in the water.

"It's a manatee," Maddie whispered hurriedly.

It was smaller than the manatees they had seen earlier. And it lacked the grace of the others in the water. It was rolling and bobbing helplessly in the tide.

"Something's wrong with it," Brandon said.

"It's acting sick," Mike observed, "just like the manta we saw."

"It's a baby," Brandon whispered. "What's it doing way out here?"

"Where are its parents?" Maddie asked.

The manatee came up for air, lifting its head above the water, but it couldn't keep its balance. It flopped sideways into the water.

"Something's really wrong," Brandon said.

"We've got to help it," Maddie announced.

"What can *we* do?" Mike asked.

Brandon looked around. "Whatever we do, we've got to be quiet. That guy is still out there."

"We should take it to Doc Hastings," Maddie said. "He'll know what to do."

"How are we going to do that?" Mike asked.

"I know how," Brandon said as he began

rummaging at the stern of the dinghy. After a few moments he had assembled the gear that he needed. He had a large net and several pieces of rope. "I'll get the manatee into the net and we'll drag it back to Doc's place."

"Can't we just bring it on board?" Maddie asked.

"Too big for that," Brandon replied. "It would sink the dinghy."

Brandon took off his shirt and slipped quietly over the side into the water. He held onto the boat until his feet touched bottom. When he stood, the water only came up to his chest.

He made his way toward the baby manatee, stepping carefully to avoid tripping on any roots or rocks.

The manatee didn't even seem to notice when Brandon slipped the net over it. Brandon drew the ropes from the net under the manatee and lifted it slightly out of the water. The manatee took a deep breath and moved its flippers weakly, but otherwise it was quiet.

Mike and Maddie used the oars to push the dinghy closer to Brandon and the manatee. Brandon grabbed hold of the side of the dinghy and handed the ropes from the net to Mike. Then he climbed back aboard and put on his shirt.

The roar of a powerful engine filled the night.

Maddie and Mike both had the same thought. The man in the boat had seen them and was coming to get them!

CHAPTER
14

The roar became louder, then began to diminish. The speedboat was moving away from them.

Brandon waited until the sound of the speedboat had disappeared. Then he started the small outboard. Keeping it at very low power, he edged the dinghy out of the mangroves and into open water. The manatee trailed behind, floating in the net.

"Look!" Maddie said. "The lights are gone."

"That's probably why that guy took off," Mike added. "Whew!" he continued, "something stinks."

"Maybe it's the sick manatee," Maddie said. She looked back at Brandon. He was slumping over the outboard motor. "Are you okay?"

Brandon lifted his head weakly. "Yeah. I don't know. . . I just feel a little cold, but I can get us to

Doc's." He steered the dinghy toward Caye Caulker, moving slowly to avoid injuring the baby manatee they were dragging behind.

Mike sat in the bow of the boat looking out for rocks or coral. Maddie sat in the back next to Brandon. She kept her eyes on the manatee, making sure it was all right.

The baby manatee bobbed along behind them in the net. Maddie could see that its eyes were open and that it seemed to be breathing, but she couldn't hear any sounds from it because of the noise of the outboard motor. Then she heard a louder, deeper roaring.

Maddie looked back and saw a speedboat coming from the direction of the reef, heading directly for them. "Brandon!" she shouted.

Brandon had seen it, too. He swung the outboard motor hard to the side, turning the dinghy sharply. But the weight of the manatee held them back. The speedboat was surely going to hit them.

Brandon gunned the outboard, but it was still moving too slowly. The speedboat bore down on them. At the last moment the speedboat swerved away, passing a few feet behind them. Its deck was brightly lit and crowded with men. Maddie thought she saw a blue and red T-shirt.

"They didn't see us," Mike said

"They might not have even noticed us if they hit us," Brandon added, "just like a manatee."

"We'd better check out the little manatee," Maddie said.

They stopped the dinghy and Brandon went into the water to check on the manatee. It was still feeble, but it seemed okay. Brandon got back in the dinghy and steered for shore.

The outboard motor was laboring, coughing and sputtering occasionally because of the load it was pulling. At times it seemed that they weren't making any headway, but the mangrove island receded into the darkness and the lights on Caye Caulker began to grow.

Maddie noticed that Brandon was scratching his back. "Are you really okay?" she asked.

"Something's making my skin itch," Brandon replied. "It feels like it's burning." He held his hand up and looked at it. "What is this stuff?" His hand was coated with sticky stuff that glistened in the moonlight.

"Hold the throttle," Brandon said. He got his flashlight and pointed it at his hand. The stuff was colorless but it made his skin look slick and greasy. He shined the light on his legs. They were coated, too.

Brandon tried to rub it off. "What is this stuff?" he asked again. There was an edge to his voice. He held his hand under his nose and turned quickly away. "Gross! That's what smells so bad."

Mike came back from the bow. "Maybe you can rub it off with my towel," he said as he handed it to Brandon.

Brandon took the towel and rubbed his leg. He winced in pain. "It's not working. I feel like I'm on fire!" His skin was turning red like a sunburn.

Maddie kept steering the boat toward the lights of Caye Caulker. "Do you have a first-aid kit?" she asked.

Brandon shook his head. "I don't feel so good now," he said.

"Maybe it's a jellyfish," Mike suggested.

Brandon shook his head again. "I've had jellyfish stings before. They don't leave gooey stuff on you. This is way worse. " He crouched by the side of the dinghy. "I think I'm gonna be sick."

Mike looked at Maddie. "What should we do?"

"Get him to Doc Hastings," she replied.

"Maybe we should cut the manatee loose."

"No way . . . don't do it," Brandon said. He was shivering now, as though he had a chill. "We've got to save it."

"Is there anything we can cover him up with to keep him warm?" Maddie asked.

Mike looked around. There was nothing. "All we can do is get him to shore."

They were close enough to Caye Caulker now so they could make out the individual houses.

"Look for a big green pole with a yellow light on top," Brandon said unsteadily. "That'll be the dock for Doc's place."

Brandon lay down in the bottom of the boat and closed his eyes.

Maddie steered the boat along the shore until she saw the green pole. Then she turned in and guided the dinghy next to the dock. Mike jumped up onto the dock and tied the bowline.

Maddie shut down the motor. "Go get Doc, Mike!" she cried.

She glanced down at Brandon. He looked very sick. "Come on, Brandon," she said, taking his arm. "We've got to get you on shore."

Maddie was able to get Brandon up on the dock, where he stood unsteadily. A moment later Mike appeared with Doc Hastings running right behind, holding his old fishing hat on with one hand.

"What's going on?" Doc said. "What are you three doing out at this hour?" Then he saw Brandon. "Let's get you inside," he said, grabbing Brandon around the waist. "From the look of it, you need some medical attention."

Maddie and Mike started to follow when Maddie heard a faint splash. "Oh, my gosh, Mike!"

she exclaimed. "We completely forgot about the baby manatee."

"Doc," Mike called. "We found a baby manatee. What should we do with it?"

"You have it here?" Doc asked in disbelief.

"We brought it in a net," Maddie replied.

"Well, see if you two can get it out of the net and into one of the pens."

"It's sick, Doc," Brandon said weakly.

"I've got to take care of you first," Doc said to Brandon. "Then I'll look after the manatee."

Mike and Maddie climbed back into the dinghy and started to untie the ropes holding the net with the baby manatee.

"Have you got any idea what we're doing?" Mike asked.

"Nope," Maddie replied. "I guess we'll just have to do the best we can."

It turned out to be easier than they expected, but both twins had to go into the water. Although the baby manatee struggled a little as they worked it out of the net, it calmed down once it was free of it. The baby manatee was very gentle. Maddie simply opened the door to one of the floating pens and Mike guided it in.

The baby manatee was still swimming unsteadily, but it headed directly to the fence that separated it from another enclosure where two adult manatees were held. As Mike and Maddie watched, the two adults swam over next to the baby manatee. The baby surfaced and took a deep breath. It sounded like a sigh and echoed in the night.

Mike turned to Maddie and gave her a high five. Then they went to check on Brandon.

CHAPTER 15

Brandon seemed to be feeling better when the twins got up to Doc's house. He was wrapped in a blanket, sitting at Doc's large kitchen table.

"He made me take a shower and scrub with this real rough soap," Brandon said irritably.

"He had to get that gunk off him, whatever it was," Doc said. "I made him wash up thoroughly."

"I must have picked it up when I went in the water," Brandon said.

The twins looked at each other.

"We just got out of the water," Maddie said with some alarm in her voice.

"Do you think we got any of that stuff on us," Mike added, looking at his arms and legs.

"No," Brandon replied. "I think it happened out

by the reef." He seemed to be back to his old self. "What happened to the baby manatee?"

"We put him in the pen," Mike responded, "just like Doc told us."

"He swam over to some other manatees in the pen next door," Mike continued. "He looks like he's going to be okay."

"The water around here looks pretty clean," Doc added. "Those sick manatees seem to recover nicely from whatever is wrong with them."

"Do you think what made Brandon sick is making the sea animals sick?" Maddie asked

Doc shook his head thoughtfully. "I don't know, Maddie. That's as good a guess as any. I just can't be sure." He lifted his tattered hat and scratched his head. "This is very strange. . . ."

They waited for Doc to continue, but he seemed lost in thought.

Finally he spoke. "I haven't seen anything like this in years, not since I was in World War II in the Pacific. . . ." He trailed off again.

"What was it, Doc?" Brandon asked.

"It was really a fluke," Doc said. "The war was almost over and I was on a destroyer in the South Pacific. We heard a distress call and when we investigated we found a Japanese submarine wallowing in the water. Some of our guys thought it was a trick, but most of the submarine's crew were in life rafts or floating in the ocean. We picked them up and took them aboard. Some of them had burns like Brandon's, only much more serious."

"Then what happened?" Mike asked.

"A party of our guys went over to the submarine. When they came back, some of them had burns, too, but nothing like the Japanese. We treated them the best we could. We tried a lot of ointments and medicine, but hot water and soap seemed to work best."

"What caused it?" Maddie inquired.

"That took a little figuring out," Doc replied. "You see, in World War II submarines used big stacks of batteries to supply power while they were submerged. Most batteries produce electricity by putting metal in contact with acid. This submarine was trying out some sort of advanced batteries with a very powerful acid. Somehow the acid got loose in the submarine. The crew tried flooding the battery compartment, but that only spread the acid. So they abandoned ship.

"I found out later that we'd tried the same thing on our submarines but decided it was too risky for the crew. Sailors got burned. You wouldn't want that stuff around when somebody was shooting at you. I can't believe anybody uses batteries like that nowadays." Doc shook his head. "That acid would be pretty dangerous if it got loose in the environment. But I can't imagine that what's happened to Brandon has anything to do with battery acid."

"Doc," Brandon said, "I'm feeling okay now. Can we take a look at the baby manatee?" He stood up and walked toward the door.

"Sure," Doc replied. "Let's take a look."

The twins followed Brandon and Doc out to the floating pens. At first they couldn't find the baby manatee, but some telltale bubbles showed that it was still in the corner of the pen where the twins had left it. Soon it rose to the surface of the water to take a breath. Two other manatees in the adjacent pen surfaced at the same time. They could hear the manatees inhale, and then they sank out of sight again.

Doc studied the baby manatee closely, watching it surface and submerge several times. Finally he spoke. "It looks like it's behaving pretty naturally now. None of that shaking or clumsy swimming like some of the adults I've had here."

"Maybe the boat trip was good for it," Maddie suggested.

"Sure, Maddie," Mike said sarcastically, "getting dragged behind a boat is my idea of a magic cure."

Brandon laughed.

Maddie felt her face turning red. "No, no," she

said. "I mean that pulling the baby manatee through the water might have had the same effect as Brandon's taking a shower."

"The water washed away whatever was causing the problem," Doc said, continuing Maddie's thought. "That's very smart, Maddie."

Brandon and Mike stopped laughing and looked a little embarrassed.

"You kids have given me the first real clue to the mystery of what is happening on the reef," Doc said. "I think whatever made Brandon sick is what's making the fish sick. It's something in the water, like that battery acid."

"But where would it come from?" Mike asked.

"I don't know," Doc replied, "but I aim to find out. If that's the problem, then we can do something about it."

"Can we help?" Maddie asked.

"Yes, I think you can," Doc answered. "I'm going out on the reef tomorrow to take a look around. I'd like you kids to come along and show me where you found this baby manatee. There might be more out there that need rescuing."

"And," said Mike, "we might find more clues to this mystery!"

CHAPTER
16

"Was your dad mad last night?" Mike asked Brandon as they walked toward Doc's place the next morning.

"No," Brandon responded. "Doc called him and told him what we'd found. Dad was more interested in asking me questions about last night than he was in getting mad. How 'bout you?"

"Our dad was okay, too," Maddie replied. "He was on the phone with Doc when we came in."

"Jenna was there, too," Mike added.

"Yeah," Maddie continued, "but she wasn't mad, either. She just seemed glad that we were okay."

"My dad's going out to the reef with us,"

Brandon said. "Doc invited him."

"Doc invited our dad, too," Mike responded, "but he can't come. He's got a survey to finish before tomorrow. But Jenna said she might come."

"She won't show up," Maddie declared. "She's too involved with the wedding plans."

"I wouldn't bet on it," Brandon said.

• • •

Jenna was standing on Doc's porch talking with him and Jim Shaw when the twins and Brandon arrived.

Doc's motorboat was bigger than most of the others the twins had seen. It had a large square cut out of the bottom that was covered with glass. When they looked through it, they could see the bottom of the ocean clearly below them. The twins watched as they headed out to the small island they had visited the night before, but they couldn't see much when the boat was moving fast.

"Not much happening, Doc," Brandon's father said. The surface of the ocean was quiet and smooth. Besides a few seagulls that followed them for a while, there was little to see except the reflection of the hot sun.

As they approached the mangroves surrounding the small island, Doc slowed the boat and steered carefully along the shore. Through the glass bottom they could see the coral reefs. At first the reefs were teeming with life. They could see brightly colored fish dodging among the coral outcrops, fleeing the shadow of the boat as it came by.

"Our boat was tied up along here somewhere," Brandon said. "The other boat was anchored somewhere over there."

"The boat with Jenna's brother," Maddie whispered to Mike. He nodded.

"You're sure this is the place where the boat was tied up?" Brandon's father asked.

"Pretty sure," Brandon replied. "It looked different at night."

"Wow!" Mike declared. "Look at that." He pointed at the glass bottom.

Several fish were in view and they were swimming crazily, rubbing against the coral and almost spinning in the water. The coral had changed, too. It was bleached white and dead looking. And much of it was covered with dark brown mud.

Doc stopped the boat and threw out the anchor. "We need some samples," he said.

"We'll get you some," Brandon volunteered. He and his father put on their masks and fins.

"Be careful," Doc said. "The current is very strong here. It seems to be coming from the direction of Lighthouse Reef."

"That's where those weird lights were, remember?" Mike whispered to Maddie.

Brandon and his father dropped over the side of the boat into the water. They adjusted their snorkels and began diving for samples. They each had small buckets to hold samples of the sand and coral, and small nets to catch some of the spinning fish.

After a short while, they swam back to the boat and handed the samples up to Doc.

Brandon took the snorkel out of his mouth. "Dad," he said, "I feel that same stinging I felt last night."

"I feel it, too," Brandon's father replied

"You'd better get out right now," Doc said emphatically. "I prepared for something like this."

Brandon and his father climbed onto the stern of the boat and took off their masks and fins.

"Just stay right there," Doc said. He handed Jenna a hose and went into the cabin. A moment later they could hear the sound of a small pump. Then Doc turned some valves on a large tank in the front of the boat. Suddenly a weak stream of water squirted out of the hose Jenna was holding.

"Wait a minute," Doc called. He adjusted the valves and the water began to flow much faster.

Jenna aimed the stream of water at Brandon and his father, washing them down as they turned around.

"I think that's enough," Brandon's father finally said. Maddie handed both of them towels and they began to dry off.

"I don't know which was worse," Brandon's father said, "the stinging or that cold water."

"I can tell you, Dad," Brandon responded. "The stinging gets much worse if you don't get it off right away."

Doc was leaning over the side and filling glass jars with seawater. "I want to get these back to my place as quickly as we can," he said. "Whatever it is, I need my lab to figure it out."

As the boat headed back to shore, they passed a school of torpedolike tarpon. The fish were swimming in all directions, jumping out of the water and bumping and rubbing against each other.

Brandon's father scratched his head. "I've never seen anything like it," he said.

When they got back to shore, Doc collected the samples to take to his house.

"If you don't mind, Doc," Jenna said, "I'd like to take a few of these to a friend of mine who's a chemist."

"Sure," Doc replied, handing her some of the bottles. "I can use all the help I can get."

Jenna walked away, cradling the bottles in her arms.

"I'll bet she's going to give those to her brother," Maddie whispered to Mike. "We can't trust her."

"Give me a break," Mike whispered back. "She's cool."

"We'll see," Maddie said.

"Hey," Brandon said, "let's check out the baby manatee."

The baby manatee swam over to them when they reached the pen. It seemed healthy and swam easily, staying near the surface where they could see it clearly.

"Wow," Mike remarked. "That's a change."

The manatee paused and lifted its head out of the water. It seemed to be looking straight at them. "It's like it's glad to see us," Brandon said. Then the baby manatee flipped over and swam back toward the side of the pen where the other manatees were.

"I've got an idea," Brandon said. He went over to the end of the pier and came back with a hose. "If this makes the baby feel as good as it made me," he said as he turned on the fresh water, "that'll be one happy manatee."

Brandon directed the stream of fresh water on a spot in the pen near where they stood. The water splashed loudly as it struck the surface of the ocean. The baby manatee swam over to look, but as soon as the water hit it's body, it turned away.

"You're spraying it too hard," Maddie said. "Let me try."

She took the hose from Brandon and used her thumb to turn the hard stream into a spray. The manatee came toward them again to investigate, but this time it didn't swim away. It moved into the spray, playfully turning around as though it was trying to let the spray wash every part of it.

"It likes the spray," Mike said excitedly. Maddie and Brandon agreed.

Then the baby manatee turned on its back and floated on the surface, letting the spray roll over its stomach. It flapped its flippers against the water and made a big splash with its big round tail.

"It's almost like it's laughing," Maddie observed.

"Maybe it's ticklish," Mike said.

"Manatees are more like us than I thought," said Brandon, sounding surprised as he watched the manatee squirm. "This is really awesome."

CHAPTER
17

It was after dusk when Doc finally appeared. The twins and Brandon had spent the day watching the manatees and cleaning and refueling the motor of Brandon's dinghy. Then they went swimming at the cut near the north end of Caye Caulker. Doc seemed very excited as he came up onto the twins' deck.

"Would you like a soda?" Jenna asked.

"A soda would be great," Doc replied. "I think I've discovered what's causing the problem on the reef."

"What is it, Doc?" Maddie asked.

"I got on the Internet and contacted some of my friends. One of them suggested I look into some papers that have just been declassified by the U. S. government."

"You mean spy stuff?" Mike asked.

"No," Doc replied, "not really. Just some old records from the end of World War II they never got around to releasing before. My friend said it was funny that I called him. Someone else had asked him about the same papers a few months ago, but he couldn't remember the name."

Jenna handed Doc a cold soda and he took a long drink before he began to speak.

"That led me to some stuff on the Web in Japan. I called another old friend to see if he could help. He put me in touch with a professor in Tokyo who worked for the Japanese Navy during World War II. We talked and it turned out that we even served in the same places, on opposite sides, of course. We were both at . . ."

"Doc," Steve Richards broke in, "tell us about the reef."

"Oh, yes," Doc replied. "I was coming to that."

Doc sat for a moment collecting his thoughts. "You're not going to believe the story I got from Japan. It sounds impossible."

"Just tell us, Doc," Jenna suggested.

"It seems that near the end of World War II," Doc began, "some of the Japanese leaders realized that they were going to lose the war. So they set up a plan to establish the Japanese emperor in exile. They decided that the best place to hide would be deep in the interior of South America. They planned to sneak the emperor and his family out of Japan by boat or airplane, but the war ended too soon for them to put the plan into action."

"I don't understand," Brandon said. "What does this have to do with the fish on our reef?"

"Yeah," Mike agreed.

"Just a minute," Doc replied. "I'll get to it. These officials decided that they had to purchase land and supplies in South America to set up a place suitable for the Emperor. So, they took a huge quantity of gold from the national treasury and put it aboard a submarine, one of their huge I-class boats. I-class submarines were longer than a football field and faster than any submarine at the time. They were so big that they could carry midget submarines or even launch airplanes. At one time there was even a plan to use I-class subs to launch an air attack on the Panama Canal, but it never came off. A Japanese pilot did bomb part of the forest in Oregon in 1942 using a plane launched from a submarine. The bombs started some fires, but luckily they burned themselves out."

"Doc, please come to the point," Steve Richards said. "Tell us about the reef."

"Oh, yes, the reef," Doc said, adjusting his glasses. "The submarine with the gold was supposed to sail up the Orinoco River and leave the gold with some agents of the Japanese government. The Orinoco is in Venezuela. The land around it was pretty undeveloped at the time.

"Unfortunately, they lost contact with the submarine and it disappeared. Those few people who knew about the plan thought that it was probably sunk in the Pacific, but these papers from the U.S. Navy tell a different story. It may be that the submarine ran aground on the reefs off Belize and sunk there."

"But what has this got to do with the fish, Doc?" Brandon asked.

"It's what I saw last night, Brandon. I told you that your skin looked like it had been irritated by acid, just like those sailors I saw years ago."

"Yeah," Brandon said, nodding.

"The acid may be coming from the sunken Japanese submarine."

"No," Steve Richards said. "That's not possible. Why would we find acid in the water now if the sub sunk years ago?"

"Maybe something disturbed the wreck," Doc went on.

Maddie was a little bored by this talk of submarines, and she wandered over to the edge of the deck and gazed out to sea. She started to figure out what time it was back home and what Mom would be doing right now.

Jenna followed and stood beside her. "Is everything all right, Maddie?" she asked.

Maddie nodded. "Yeah."

"I really like you, Maddie," Jenna said. "I hope we're going to be friends."

Maddie thought she and Jenna might eventually have a talk like this, and she was kind of dreading it. Still, she liked Jenna enough to listen to what she had to say.

"Your father is very important to both of us. I really want him to be happy." Maddie listened. "You're very important to him, Maddie," Jenna continued. "If you're not happy, he won't be. So I'd like to do what I can to be your friend."

After a long pause Maddie turned to Jenna. "Okay," she said, "we can try."

"Would you like to be my maid of honor?" Jenna asked.

Maddie was surprised but also kind of excited. "Really?" she asked.

"Yes," Jenna said. "It would mean a lot to me if you would consider it."

"Sure...okay...I'll do it," Maddie responded. She turned back toward the ocean.

"We'll talk about it some more later," Jenna said.

Something caught Maddie's eye. A light flashed near Lighthouse Reef. She ran over to her father. "Dad! Look!" she said.

"What is it, Maddie?" her father asked.

"The lights are back," Maddie said, pointing out to sea. "Look there."

"I saw it, too," Jenna added.

There was another bright flash, followed by two more.

"C'mon," Maddie's father said. "Let's get my boat and find out what those lights are all about."

He led the way down to the dock where his boat was tied. Doc and Jenna got aboard while he untied the lines to the boat. "Look," the twins' father said, "you kids stay with Brandon. This could be danger-ous and I don't want anything to happen to you." He climbed aboard the boat and pushed off. "We'll be back soon," he called as he started the boat's engine.

Maddie was very disappointed. "It's our mys-tery, too," she said.

"Yeah," Mike agreed, "we're the ones who saw the lights first." He looked dejected, too.

"Well," Brandon said brightly, "you'll just have to do what your dad said."

"Why are you so happy?" Mike snapped.

"Because," Brandon replied, "your dad said you have to stay with me. And I am going to get into my dinghy and go see what's going on out there."

"Yes!" both twins exclaimed.

CHAPTER
18

Brandon guided the dinghy around the end of the small island they had visited the night before. He shut off the outboard motor. All three teens crouched down in the dinghy as they drifted in the darkness toward Lighthouse Reef.

Brandon stuck his head up and looked through a small pair of binoculars he had brought along.

"Can you see anything?" Maddie whispered.

"Not really, but I think I know why we couldn't see much before," he replied. "Here," he said, handing the binoculars to Maddie. "Take a look."

Maddie scanned across the horizon, but she could see very little. There seemed to be nothing but dark ocean and the star-filled sky.

"Look right there," Brandon suggested, pointing.

Maddie focused the binoculars. She noticed that there were no stars along one part of the horizon. It looked like there were some shadows that were darker than the sky. Then she recognized them as boats.

"They've got some sort of screen to keep us from seeing the lights," Brandon said.

"Yeah," Maddie agreed. "I can barely see it. It's like they hung a curtain between the boats."

"Let me see," Mike insisted. Maddie handed him the glasses.

"Somebody doesn't want anyone to know what's going on," Brandon said, "but if we can get closer, maybe we can find out what's happening."

"If they don't want people to see what's going on," Maddie suggested, "maybe it's dangerous. Maybe they're doing something illegal."

"There's something above the screen," Mike said. "It looks like the top of a crane."

"Where?" Maddie asked.

Mike handed her the glasses and pointed.

"I can see it without the glasses," Brandon said. "Let's go closer and get a better view."

Brandon started the outboard and guided the dinghy in a wide circle around the crane and the boats. As they came around, they could see gaps in the screen that allowed light to come through.

"It looks like they were mostly worried about

people on land seeing what they were doing," Brandon said as he shut down the motor again. "They don't seem worried about anyone seeing them from this side."

"Maybe they thought the reef would keep people away," Mike suggested.

"Maybe," Brandon replied.

They watched as the current slowly carried them toward the boats and the bright lights. Through the break in the screen, they could see a large crane on a barge and several smaller boats with bright spotlights illuminating the area. Behind the crane a row of sailboats with tall masts held up huge pieces of cloth, forming the screen that kept the crane from being seen from land.

"It *is* like a curtain," Maddie said.

"Something that big must be hard to control," Mike added.

"That's why we saw those flashes from home," Brandon said. "The curtain must slip sometimes."

The crane seemed to be straining as it tried to pull something out of the ocean. The barge it was on was tilting as though the crane was lifting a heavy weight. One side was almost underwater.

"It looks like some kind of salvage operation," Mike remarked.

"Maybe they've found pirate treasure or something dangerous," Maddie speculated.

"Whatever it is, it must be heavy," Brandon said, "and they must be going deep. My dad said the ocean bottom drops off at the edge of the reef more than three thousand feet down along here."

The crane began to sway. They could hear it now, the low rumble of its engine rose in pitch until it was a roar.

"They've definitely got something!" Mike said excitedly.

The barge the crane was on tipped even more. Now they could see the cable from the arm of the crane slowly reeling in. Water dripped off the cable as it rose.

"What's that?" Maddie asked.

A large black shape slowly rose out of the deep and broke the surface. It appeared to be some kind of ship. In the bright light they could see that it was streaked with rust. One end of the shape rose higher out of the water. It looked like the pointed bow of a submarine.

"Doc was right," Maddie said in astonishment.

The noise from the crane suddenly changed. There was a cracking sound, like sticks of wood breaking, and a shrieking whine of the motor straining. The barge tipped further, its back end coming out of the water. Some men appeared on the barge, running around in some kind of panic. One of them dove off the barge and swam toward a nearby boat.

With the sound of twisting metal and a sharp snap, the arm of the crane bent downward and the cable lifting the submarine came apart. The crane reared up and the barge tipped backward. It looked like it was going to capsize, but with a great splash it slammed forward again and rocked back and forth.

The rusty bow of the submarine paused for a moment in the water and then, with a froth of huge bubbles, it sank back into the depths.

"Hold on," Brandon shouted.

A huge wave caused by the barge slamming against the water was rushing toward them. It crashed into the sides of the dinghy, shaking and buckling the rubber boat. Water poured in.

The dinghy was going to sink!

CHAPTER
19

The dinghy rocked back and forth and water rolled over its sides, flowing into the bottom. Mike and Maddie tried to scoop the water out with their hands, but it was coming in too fast.

"We're sinking!" Maddie cried.

"No, we're not," Brandon said. He grabbed a small bucket and began to bail. "Keep the boat steady," he ordered. "If we can stop the water from coming over the sides, we'll be okay. We can bail out what's already inside."

More big waves from the barge slapped against the sides of the dinghy, but Mike and Maddie balanced the boat against the waves and tried to keep it steady. Slowly the waves subsided and the dinghy stopped rocking.

Brandon was making some headway with his bailing and gradually the level of the water inside the boat went down.

"Whew!" Brandon said after a few more minutes of bailing. "That was close."

The dinghy was steady now and, although all three teens were soaked, everyone was okay.

"Now let me see if I can get the motor started," Brandon said.

"Hey, look!" Mike exclaimed. "Something's happening to the crane."

They had floated much closer to the large crane. When they looked they could see that it was almost surrounded by small boats with red and blue flashing lights.

"It's the police and the Belize Coast Guard," Brandon said. "Look, there's my dad's boat."

One of the police boats turned and came toward them with its lights flashing.

"They've seen us," Mike said. "We're busted."

The glare of a spotlight nearly blinded them as a police boat approached.

"Ahoy, dinghy," a man's voice shouted. "Take hold of this line and prepare to come aboard."

A line snapped across the bow of the dinghy and Maddie grabbed it. Brandon took it from her and tied it to an oarlock. The line tightened and the dinghy was pulled alongside the police boat. Strong arms reached down in the glare and pulled them aboard.

"Turn off the spot," a man ordered. The spotlight went out.

As her eyes adjusted to the dark, Maddie realized that she recognized the man giving the orders. "It's him!" she whispered to Mike.

"You three don't look any the worse for wear," Jenna's brother, Tim, said with a smile. "You okay?"

The three teens nodded.

The boat turned and moved toward the other police boats that were gathered around the wrecked crane. Several policemen were taking the crew of the crane prisoner. A group of them walked past the teens with their hands on their heads. Maddie suddenly realized the man in the blue and red T-shirt from the ferry was among them.

"You got here just in time to see the end of our investigation," Tim said. "We caught these guys red-handed."

As they neared the barge, Maddie saw her father and Doc standing next to the crane. The crane arm was bent near the middle and the metal struts were twisted and broken. Brandon's father was also nearby, directing some rangers who were inspecting the damage.

"Well," Doc said when he saw the three, "I

knew you couldn't stay away."

The twins' father scowled and started to say something, but Doc spoke first. "Don't blame them," he said. "I don't think I could have stayed away either when I was their age. If it weren't for them, we never would have put all the pieces together. They ought to be congratulated."

"I guess Doc's right," her father said. "You kids provided the key clue that solved the mystery of what was going on out here."

The three looked at each other in surprise. "Which clue?" Maddie asked.

"When you brought Brandon to Doc," Mr. Richards said, "he guessed that someone was trying to raise an old wreck out on the reef."

"I was right about what made Brandon sick," Doc added. "It was acid from the batteries in that sunken submarine. Apparently these men found out about the submarine from those same navy papers I read, only they were a few months ahead of me. If it hadn't been for my friend telling me about those papers, I might never have figured it out."

Steve Richards continued, "The samples we took showed that Doc's suspicions were right. When they tried to raise the sunken submarine, these crooks broke open the battery compartment and released large quantities of battery acid into the sea.

That's what was making the fish act so crazy."

"And that's why dragging the baby manatee behind my boat seemed to make it act better," Brandon said.

"The water washed the acid off it," Maddie added.

"It was just like the shower I gave Brandon," Doc said.

"But what about the fish now?" Mike asked.

"Yeah, Mike," Maddie continued the thought. "The submarine is still down there. Won't it keep leaking acid into the water?"

"Won't the fish keep getting sick?" Brandon added.

"No," Doc replied, "the tide will wash the acid away and dilute it so much that it will no longer be a threat. The manatees can go back to their feeding grounds and the fish should be all right. Sometimes nature is the best healer."

"And now we have these guys under arrest for polluting and illegal treasure hunting," Jenna's brother, Tim, broke in.

"But *who* are you?" Maddie asked in exasperation. "Are you really Jenna's brother?"

"Tim *is* Jenna's brother *and* an undercover agent for the Belize police," her father said. "Jenna took those samples to him and he set up this raid."

A police officer in uniform came up to Tim. "Our sonar can't locate the sub, sir. It must have slipped all the way down to the bottom. That's beyond the range of our equipment."

"Thank you," Tim replied. He turned back to the teens. "You see, the only reason there was any chance of raising the submarine was because it was stuck on a ledge on the reef only a few hundred feet down. Now it's gone all the way to the bottom, more than three thousand feet down. You'll need some really expensive equipment just to find it again, let alone bring it up."

"If it *is* an I-class submarine," Doc said, "it could weigh over three thousand tons. That's why this crane broke trying to lift it out of the water. It was too heavy."

"But what about the Japanese gold?" Maddie asked.

"We aren't even sure that there really is any gold aboard that submarine," Doc said. "Now it's sunk so deep it may never be recovered and we'll never find out."

CHAPTER
20

"That wasn't as bad as I expected," Mike said to Maddie and Brandon. They were seated at a large round table at the outdoor wedding reception.

Maddie was much more enthusiastic. "It was beautiful," she insisted. "The flowers, the music—everything was perfect." The wedding had been held outside in a lush tropical garden. Thick green foliage formed a background for pink and white blossoms on the bushes below. Other bright red and orange flowers cascaded from vines overhead.

During the ceremony Mike had stood beside his father and Maddie was next to Jenna. After they returned from the reef, she and Jenna had stayed up late, talking about lots of things. Maddie decided that Jenna wasn't so bad after all. In fact, she thought she would like to get to know her better. And after spending the past week with Dad and Jenna, Maddie knew that Jenna made her father very happy. He seemed much less lonely than he had been down here in Belize, so far from the rest of his family.

"You still embarrassed about almost blowing it?" Brandon asked Mike. "I've never seen anyone turn so red."

Mike *had* almost totally blown it when he was asked for the ring, but he managed to find it deep in the pocket where he had put it for safekeeping. Maddie had given him one of her worst looks, but Mike was only able to shrug and blush. Mike blushed again just remembering the close call.

The reception was held in another garden with tables set under tall palm trees. Brandon and the twins sat at a table with Doc Hastings and Brandon's parents.

The bride and groom walked over to their table holding hands. "Beautiful day, beautiful wedding, and beautiful bride," Doc said, leaning back from the table.

"Thank you," Jenna said graciously, "but all anybody seems to be talking about is the submarine, the manatees, and the three young detectives." She smiled and winked at Mike and Maddie. "They sort of upstaged the wedding!"

"It's about the biggest thing that's happened

around here in years," Brandon's father said, with a laugh.

"People will be talking about it for a long time to come," Doc added.

Jenna's brother, Tim, appeared and wound his way past the other tables toward them. Maddie inspected him carefully as he came nearer. She still wasn't sure whether she liked him or not, although he looked better than he had last night. He was clean shaven and wearing a white suit with a bright print shirt.

"I've got some news about the submarine," Tim said.

"See what I mean?" Jenna responded. "Even my own brother can't talk about anything else."

Tim smiled and gave his sister a kiss on the cheek. "Sorry, Sis, you're a beautiful bride. And this guy," he said, putting his hand on Steve Richard's shoulder, "is going to make a great brother-in-law."

"Thank you," Jenna responded. "Now, what about the submarine?"

"The Japanese government heard about what happened," Tim said. "They're very interested in seeing what we found."

"And lost," Doc broke in.

"They're sending a special deep-sea submersible from Japan," Tim continued, "to help search for the submarine. They want to recover the lost gold. It belongs to them anyway."

"If it's really there," the twins' father remarked.

"And the Japanese want your team to work with them," Tim said to Steve Richards. "They need an experienced engineer who knows these waters."

"Is that true?" Jenna asked.

"Yes, it is," Tim responded with a grin. "And I can hardly wait to start working with your new husband."

"You're involved, too?" Jenna asked.

"Yes, but it gets even better," Tim turned toward the teens. "The Japanese said that you kids can take a dive in the deep-sea submersible when it gets here. It's kind of a reward for the work you did."

"But we're suppose to go home next week," Maddie moaned.

"It's okay, Maddie. Your mom and I have agreed that you and Mike can visit me several times a year," the twins' father said. "We'll just have to work out the timing of your next visit once we know when the submersible will arrive."

"Awesome!" Mike, Maddie, and Brandon said at the same time.

"I thought only the twins spoke at the same time," Doc remarked. "Now we've got triplets!"

"We can start doing a little looking on our own

tomorrow," Brandon said "I know some neat places to snorkel that we haven't explored yet."

"Not tomorrow," Doc Hastings responded. "We've got a little job to do first."

"Job?" Mike protested. "This is supposed to be our vacation."

"We want to go snorkeling," Maddie added.

"Okay," Doc said, "but this might be something you'll all like."

"What kind of a job is it, Doc?" Brandon asked.

"Now that the water is clear," Doc explained, "we'll return the manatees to their home waters. I can't do it without you kids, and I wouldn't want to. You're the three best assistants this old man's ever had. And we've got to solve another little mystery."

"What's that, Doc?" Maddie asked eagerly.

"We've got to help that baby manatee find its mother. Are you interested?"

The three teens looked at each other. "Yes!" they all said at once.

AFTERWORD

Belize is a small country, but it contains a variety of attractions you can visit. From around AD 300 to 900 the land was inhabited by the Maya. They left behind ruins such as Altun Ha and Caracol. Today these are open to visitors. There are also wildlife sanctuaries such as the Community Baboon Sanctuary (*baboon* is the local name for the black howler monkey) and Crooked Tree, where you can see more than 60 kinds of tropical birds and even crocodiles. But for many visitors, the major attraction in Belize is the snorkeling or scuba diving on the cayes and the Barrier Reef just off the coast.

The Barrier Reef of Belize is the second largest in the world, smaller only than the Great Barrier Reef off northern Australia. Thousands of other, smaller coral reefs dot the tropical oceans of the world. Coral reefs are one of the richest ecosystems on the planet.

The threat to the reef described in this mystery is imaginary, but many reefs are in serious danger of destruction. Imbalances created by over-fishing and by pollution are major threats, but coral has also been "mined" to build structures on land and in the sea, and fish have actually been hunted on reefs with dynamite or strong poisons.

These threats to the reefs are matched by threats to the coastal waters and wetlands in many parts of the world. In Florida, the manatee has become one of the symbols for protecting the coastal ecosystems.

Columbus was the first European to record seeing a manatee. He saw several in 1493. If they were mermaids, he wrote, he was not very impressed by their beauty. Manatees may not be beautiful to some of us, but they have a dignity and a charm that is all their own. They are perhaps the gentlest large animal on the Earth, sometimes reaching a length of 15 feet and a weight of nearly 2,000 pounds. They feed entirely on sea grasses and other plants, and tend to browse alone or in small groups.

In Belize, manatees have been protected for many years. There are an estimated 1,500 manatees in the waters off Belize, the largest population outside of the United States. Florida has the largest population, currently estimated at around 2,000, but during the summer manatees can be found as far west as Louisiana and as far north as North Carolina or Virginia. (Chessie, who is mentioned in this mystery, is a very special case. He traveled as far north as Rhode Island.)

Manatees are very slow to reproduce, having only one calf about every two years. At this rate they are barely able to keep their population steady against accidental killings by boats and other causes of death. When more than 300 manatees died in 1996, many people feared that the whole population of manatees in Florida might be at risk. Scientists now think that the cause of these deaths was a rapid spread of an algae, known as the red tide, that grows in the ocean. Red tide contains a poison that kills fish and other aquatic life, unfortunately including manatees. Many people are working to protect these marvelous animals in the United States, Belize, and throughout the world.

The treasure of gold on the sunken Japanese submarine is based on a discovery made in 1995. During World War II, the Japanese Navy included about 40 large I-class submarines. The largest I-class submarines were 394 feet long and could travel 30,000 miles without refueling. Many were used as cargo carriers to smuggle supplies past enemy ships to island forces. Some even delivered cargoes to German bases in France. One of these, I-52, was sunk by an American torpedo plane near the end of World War II. It was found recently in deep water off the Cape Verde Islands in the middle of the Atlantic. The submarine may contain as much as $25 million in gold. Plans are being made to raise it, but that will be a difficult task. It is almost 17,000 feet below the surface of the ocean and nearly 1,200 miles from the nearest land.

Although you may not be able to search for treasure in the middle of the ocean, you *can* help protect endangered species like the manatee or environments such as the coral reefs. You can find out more about manatees in books such as *Introducing the Manatee* by Warren Zciller and *Manatees and Dugongs* by John E. Reynolds III and Daniel K. Odell. Or check out the *Save the Manatee Club* on the World Wide Web at http://objectlinks.com/manatee/ or write to them at 500 N. Maitland Ave., Maitland, FL 32751. Places to look for information on coral reefs include books such as *Coral Reefs* by Les Holliday and *Rhythms of the Reef* by Rick Sammon, and many sites on the World Wide Web.

Or you can check with your school or local environmental groups to see what you can do. Even the smallest effort is worth considering.

P. J. Stray

Other Passport Mysteries you will enjoy:

Secrets in the Mayan Ruins
The Mystery of the Sea Dog's Treasure
Lost in Merlin's Castle

Passport Mysteries take you Around the World

Look for your passport
in Passport Mysteries No. 1
Secrets in the Mayan Ruins
(paperback version only)

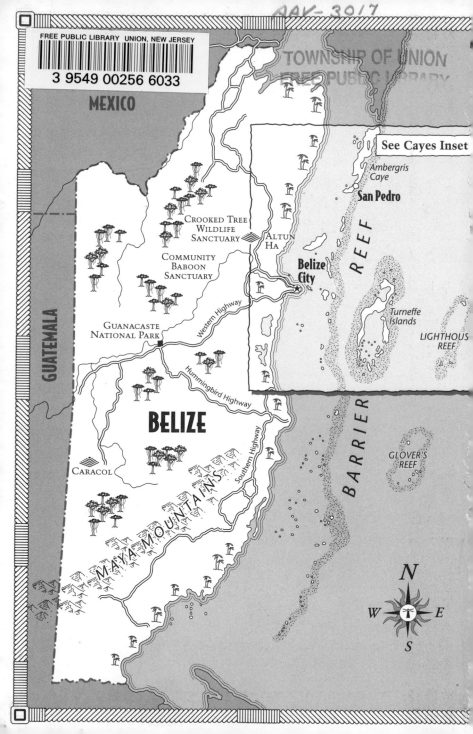

MEXICO

See Cayes Inset

Ambergris Caye

San Pedro

CROOKED TREE
WILDLIFE
SANCTUARY

ALTUN
HA

Belize City

REEF

COMMUNITY
BABOON
SANCTUARY

Western Highway

GUANACASTE
NATIONAL PARK

Turneffe Islands

LIGHTHOUSE
REEF

Hummingbird Highway

GUATEMALA

BELIZE

CARACOL

Southern Highway

GLOVER'S REEF

MAYA MOUNTAINS

BARRIER

N
W *E*
S